REASONABLE REGRET

By Mary Mack

Copyright ©2016 by Mary Mack
Printed by CreateSpace, an Amazon Company
Edited by Bev Katz Rosenbaum
Copy Edited by Deirdre Swinden
ISBN-13 978-1523694297
ISBN-10 1523694297

Acknowledgments

I would like to extend a special thank you to Hilde Alter, Deirdre Swinden and Dan "Waldo" Vitale who never stopped believing in me. And to my wonderful husband, Jim Mack; thank you for staying awake so many nights to read and re-read my never-ending drafts. To Melissa Foster, who helped me learn the ins and outs of self-publishing and marketing and to my countless friends, family and co-workers, who read my first, unpublished chapters and encouraged me to continue. And lastly, to my amazing children: Nick, Angie and Michael. Thank you for all of the love and support you have shown me through the years; it's made everything possible.

This is my first novel.

Mary Mack

*Reasonable Regret is a work of fiction.
Names, characters, places and incidents are the products of the author's imagination. Any resemblance to actual events, locales or persons living or dead is entirely coincidental.*

Dedicated to Michael

PROLOGUE

The target crosses the street, just as the midtown bus maneuvers its way up Lark Street. The bus passes – along with its curious passengers, onlookers – and the target's head is turned towards the street, his brow knitted. A millisecond later, without a trace of recognizable sound, the target is down. Dead. Stretched out on the sidewalk near the corner of Lark and Washington, a steady trickle of blood oozing from his left temple. With the greatest of ease, the shooter takes down the weapon and conceals it in its case, and strolls across the street in the opposite direction. The job here today is done; time to get home and have some lunch.

1.

I'd like to be happy. I really would. But instead I pull into the vacant lot across the street from the establishment known as the Lounge in downtown Utica and sit quietly inside of my car and wait to meet a man by the name of Carl.

It is 1:50 p.m. Carl will be here at two.

The Lounge is located in the downtown section of Utica, a dull and lifeless city situated in the southernmost section of upstate New York about fifty miles east of Syracuse. Riddled with urban decay, the city's streets are deserted, downright departed and the perfect breeding ground for the indigent and criminals alike. My fingers fumble through my giant red bag until I am certain that my envelope is still safe. I look around the empty streets. Certain no one can see me; I open the envelope and count what's inside for what must be the fiftieth time. It's all here, my life savings: ten thousand dollars, all in twenties.

I roll down the window and look around once more; the air is thick with summer rain but still no one is watching so I carefully tuck the envelope back inside my bag and begin wondering if what they say about heaven is true. Will I ever see my son, Spencer, again? Although I have never been a religious woman, today I hold on to hope that my dreams will come true. I will once again wrap my arms around him and kiss his puffy cheeks. When I close my eyes I can still picture his young face, before the cancer took away his smile and his amber eyes. Wolf eyes, the doctors called them. So gold you would think they were made of glass and so full of hope and love they could break your heart. Even when he was so utterly fatigued and lightheaded he would tell me not to worry. My little man, all grown up at the age of twelve. "Don't worry, Mom, I'll be fine," he'd say. "I'll be in remission soon. You'll see. I'll be fine."

So, for Spencer, I pretended not to worry. Even after his weight loss and the seizures. Even after the rashes and the slurred speech, even after the life support – even after he died. Then I pretended for my family. "Don't worry, I'll be fine," I told them. "God only gives you what you can handle," and all of that shit. Sure. I was fine. Adele Hamilton is always fine.

I look down at my watch. It's 1:58.

As I swing my legs out of the car and my feet hit the pavement, I notice that the rain has stopped and turned into a frayed and raveling mist. Determined, I cross the street and enter the Lounge, all alone, on a gray and dismal Thursday afternoon.

The smell of stale beer and popcorn wafts up to my nose, and I immediately feel my pulse quicken. Several neon beer signs hang above the bar: Coors, Miller Lite, Saranac and Utica Club, allowing my eyes to quickly acclimate to the dark room. Faux wood paneling encapsulates the room and is buckled and littered with tiny holes the size of misguided darts. The soles of my shoes stick to the grimy, mocha-colored carpet that covers the floor. A pool table with bright green felt seems to wait anxiously in the back room for willing patrons. Cracked and ancient black vinyl bar stools try to welcome me in. I bite. I take a seat.

"What will it be, miss?" the man behind the bar asks. He stands about five-six, about the same height as I, and wears a pre-symbol Prince tee-shirt, circa 1984, which stretches over his bulging belly. When he speaks, he runs his fingers through his blond handle-bar mustache revealing a very large and ugly tattoo on his right forearm. I snap to attention.

"I'll have a gin and tonic with two limes," I say, somewhat obediently.

"You got it, beautiful," he says with a wink, and I want to disappear but I quickly remember I'm here for a reason and let it go.

When my drink arrives, there are two lemon wedges floating around the top of my glass.

I hate lemon.

"Excuse me," I say. "Don't you have any limes?"

"No, sorry 'bout that – it was margarita night last night and they wiped me out," he explains as I fish the two lemon wedges out of my glass.

"Oh, too bad," I say and take a sip of my citrus-free drink just as another man enters the bar.

"Hi, Carl," the bartender says. "The usual?"

"Yea, Dixon," Carl says as he takes a seat next to me and looks me over. "Are you Adele?" he asks in a hoarse, cracked voice.

"Yes," I say, eying him warily.

"All right, Adele, why don't you and I take a seat in a booth, shall we?"

Carl stops at the booth closest to the pool table in the back of the room and we take our seats. Dixon delivers a shot of whiskey and a beer for Carl and I quickly take another sip of my drink. An ancient Bob Dylan song, *Lay, Lady, Lay,* begins to play from the juke-box behind the bar, and I hope I can get through this conversation in one piece.

Carl is tall, probably six-two, and middle-aged—48, I'd guess. He's not a bad-looking man, but it's obvious from the growl in his throat that he's been a smoker for many years, and judging by the natural slant of his eyes; and the way he carries himself, he has probably seen a lot of shady deals. But that's what I want, someone who knows how to get things done. "So, Adele, how can I help you?"

I stir around my drink and take another sip, happy to learn that Carl wants to get right down to business. I rehearsed for days what I would say to him once I got the chance so I waste no time on small talk. Besides, it's not my style, not since I was a little girl so I decide to dig right in, as always. "I hear from Steven in Syracuse that you might be able to help me."

"That depends, what did you have in mind?"

I look around the bar. Besides Dixon, we are all alone. "I want someone gone, forever."

"Ah, that's illegal," Carl says as he pounds back his shot. He then looks across the table, directly into my eyes, and adds, "And very expensive."

"I'm prepared," I say as I look into Carl's black eyes and return his cold, twisted smile. Upon closer inspection, Carl reminds me of Lonnie, my ex-husband. Six months after Spencer died, Lonnie announced that he'd never loved me and wanted a divorce. I could keep the house in Bayberry, he said, but he wanted out, so he left. Just like that. That was two months ago.

But I should have known.

After three years of marriage, Lonnie and I fell into an extraordinary funk. I was working forty hours a week at a job I hated; as a secretary at Carrier Corporation, in Syracuse. I also put in several long hours trying to gain some recognition hawking my jewelry line nights and weekends at local craft fairs and shopping malls. Lonnie worked forty hours per week, more or less, as a toll taker for the New York State Thruway Authority. Ironically, he was stationed in the town of Weedsport, west of Syracuse, about a twenty minute drive from our home. Lonnie spent most of his time getting stoned and listening to acid rock while he smiled and collected the tolls. Eventually this caught up with him, and he was fired. So began his endless succession of dead-end jobs.

"You must not like this person very much," Carl says as he sits back in his seat. "There's no turning back on this type of deal you know."

"I know," I say. Cool rivulets of sweat drip down the back of my neck as I hear Dixon drop more quarters into the juke-box and the song changes.

"It can be done, but, like I said, it will cost you," Carl reminds me.

"I have ten thousand dollars, no more," I say, hoping it's enough.

Carl raises his hand and asks Dixon to bring him another shot of Jack Daniels. We wait a few minutes while Dixon delivers the drink and leaves the booth again before we resume our conversation.

"Ten thousand dollars is a good amount, but it's got to be all in cash." Now Carl looks around the bar, his cold black eyes reduced to slits. "So, Adele, who is the unlucky person? An ex? An obnoxious neighbor? A relative?"

"Before I tell you, I have one stipulation," I say.

"Okay," Carl says as a genuine smile graces his face.

"I would like it done over Labor Day weekend. Any day, I don't care which, but not until then. I need some time." The Rolling Stones are trying to get some *Satisfaction* in the background as I wait for Carl's response.

Carl raises his left eyebrow as he shifts his weight in the booth. "That's a little odd. Labor Day is more than two months away. Usually these things are done right away."

"Yes, I figured as much, but this is different."

"How is it different?" Carl asks.

I lean forward in the booth and give him a long-overdue stare of my own. "Because, Carl, the person I want dead is me."

2.

Carl quickly downs his second shot and nurses his beer before giving me the slightest twinkle of continued interest. This afternoon my boutique, a Bit of Silver, is closed for the day but I'm still wearing my shop polo shirt. It is periwinkle blue and features the logo that my good friend, Deirdre, designed for me in the upper right-hand corner. The logo itself is embossed with silver foil and matches the custom-made earrings which cascade through my long blond hair.

After a long calculating look, Carl finally speaks. "Do you work for a Bit of Silver?"

"Yes, you could say that."

"What does that mean?" Carl asks. "Do you work there or don't you?"

"I own it. It's my shop," I say, flatly.

"Oh, I see….how's business?" Carl asks with a shake of his head.

"Business is good, I do all right."

Carl shifts his weight in his seat again and orders another round. Once again we wait until Dixon has delivered the drinks and left our booth before we speak. "I've got to tell ya, Adele, this isn't adding up for me," Carl says as he sips his beer.

"What do you mean?" I ask.

"What are you, thirty? Thirty-one?"

"I'm thirty-four."

"Okay, thirty-four. You're also very good looking, well-spoken and a successful business owner. I just don't get it. What's got you so twisted up inside that you think you want to die?"

"Does that matter?" I ask, although I'm not totally surprised by his question. I anticipated some resistance to my request. I pull the envelope from my bag and flash the contents in a manner so that only Carl can see the hefty stack of bills stuffed inside. I then lay the envelope with a colorful doodle of a lady bug drawn on the front, face up, next to my gin and tonic. I hope this demonstrates to him that I mean business.

"Cute lady bug," Carl says, but I understand. He wants the money.

"Thanks, they were my son's favorite," I say, immediately regretting my decision to bring up Spencer.

"*Were* his favorite?"

"Yes, *were*." I say as my cheeks flame with anger. "Listen, Carl, is all of this commentary *necessary*? Can you help me or can't you?"

"Oh, I can help you, Adele, but you'll have to excuse me while I try to figure out if you're for real or not," he says as he lights another cigarette and blows a puff of smoke out of the side of his mouth. "It's not every day that a thirty-four year old, blond beauty walks into the bar and asks me to have her killed. A person could do hard time even plotting something like this."

The pressure suddenly gets to me and I begin to tear up. I can feel the hairs on the back of my neck prickle. I want to run from the bar and forget the whole idea but I can't bear to live without my Spencer any longer. The hurt I feel inside is so intense I can't sleep, I can't eat and I no longer want to live. I've had plenty of time to think about this and I want to die so I can see my baby again, in heaven. It's a leap of faith, I know, but this is the only way I figure will work. "Listen, Carl, I have several reasons. Personal reasons. One, I don't have the nerve to kill myself. Two, I would prefer it happen when I don't see it coming. That's very important. I don't want to see the killer coming." My tears, now large and profuse, flow freely down my cheeks.

"Okay, I'm listening," Carl says as he hands me a sympathetic gaze and a napkin to dry my eyes.

"I need to sell my house and close my shop before….."

"Before Labor Day?" Carl asks.

"Right. Before Labor Day," I say. "After that I don't care how or when it happens. I just don't want to see it coming, okay? Again, that's very important." In a last ditch effort, I slide the hefty envelope over to Carl's side of the table.

He studies it for a few seconds and then says, "I'll need a picture of you and your home and work addresses."

"It's all in the envelope," I say with a sudden sense of heady anticipation followed by an awkward smile. Carl picks up the envelope and puts it into his jacket pocket, sealing our deal. I stand to leave, but before I do, I turn and ask, "Will it be you, Carl?"

"No, I'm just the go between. I take my cut, twenty percent, and then hand the rest over to…"

I put my hand up to his face. "That's okay. Please don't tell me his name. I don't want to know."

"I would never tell you the person's name, Adele, but what makes you think it's a he?" Carl asks without a hint of sarcasm.

"Good one," I say as I turn to leave the Lounge. But before I can take another step Carl asks me to wait a minute while he scribbles something down on a cocktail napkin.

"In case you change your mind," he says and hands me the napkin.

"I won't change my mind, Carl, but thanks," I say as I leave the bar, unearthed smile steady upon my face.

3.

Later that afternoon, I pull into my housing development, located in Liverpool, New York, just as yellow school bus No. 104 stops ahead of me delivering neighborhood children to their homes. Out of habit, I take a quick glance at the clock; 3:45 p.m., right on time. I stop my car and watch as Spencer's old classmates step off the bus and onto the street. Some of the children notice me and wave; their shy smiles apologize for my loss. Some, I think, pretend not to see me because seeing me reminds them that their friend is no longer here. While others, completely oblivious to me and everyone else, look up at the sky and watch as hawks circle in great lazy loops in search of their next meal.

Eleven. There should be eleven children here today. Ever since one little girl in our district, by the name of Rebecca, fell asleep on the bus and failed to come home that night, the other mothers and I got into the habit of counting heads as our children exited the bus. But today, and for the last eight months since Spencer died, there are only ten children stepping off bus No. 104 and returning home to their families.

A familiar iron fist clenches around my heart as I begin to tear up for the second time today. I watch as the children run to their homes, their colorful backpacks flapping behind them as they scurry. A moment of pure envy sweeps through me as I see mothers emerge from their front porch steps and embrace their children. I don't notice the school bus as it pulls away, nor do I hear the sound of the man behind me honking his horn encouraging me to move forward. All I hear is the echo of Spencer's laughter as he runs into my arms when suddenly, a quick, and hard pulse in my throat –

coupled with the sound of the retched horn behind me – breaks me from my spell and I regain my chilly composure. After a quick, half-hearted wave of apology to the anxious driver behind me I pull away, completely certain I want to die.

When I pull into my driveway, my cat, Wellington, is waiting for me at the living room window. Wellington is old, thirteen to be exact, but he is still a very handsome cat with charcoal gray fur and crystal green eyes. Lonnie surprised me with him as a kitten when we were first married. Six months later Spencer was born. Wellington adored the baby right from the start and kept guard outside his bedroom door. A very polite cat, Wellington would not enter Spencer's room until I stepped in first to nurse or change a diaper, and then he would enter behind me. I can't be certain, but I suspect Wellington still misses Spencer and wonders why he disappeared.

I enter the house through the garage and then the kitchen door where Wellington now waits for me. A deep, primal joy oozes from him as he rubs up against my leg and begins to purr; so happy to see me. That or he wants to be fed. Sure enough, his dish is empty. "All right, big guy," I say as I reach into the pantry and refill his fish-shaped bowl. "Here you go." Wellington is once again content.

I open the refrigerator and pull out some left over chicken salad and a fresh bottle of Riesling and sit down at the kitchen table. As I try to eat, I pull out my cell phone and scroll through the list of names until I find the number for my realtor. She answers her phone on the second ring.

"Hello, Barbara Evans, how may I help you?" Barbara has a certain grace about her. She is well known for her aggressive yet polite attitude, honesty and hardworking business ethic and, inasmuch, has been the top-selling realtor in the Syracuse region for more than twenty years. She prides herself in knowing the area well, inside and out, and knows how to sell a house, quickly; exactly what I need right now.

"Hi, Barbara, it's Adele Hamilton calling."

There is a long pause and I remember that Barbara and I have not spoken since Spencer's funeral. I'm not even sure if she's heard that Lonnie and I have split up. I wait a few seconds for her to collect her thoughts. "Oh, Adele, how are you holding up?" she asks.

"I'm fine, really I am," I say, grateful that she cannot see the lie written across my face.

"I heard about you and Lonnie. Oh, honey, I'm so sorry."

"Please, Barbara, don't be. Lonnie and I were never right for each other and then after Spencer..." my voice begins to crack but Barbara rescues me.

"Don't say another word, Adele. You are right. Lonnie was never good enough for you, everyone could see that. You're better off on your own, you'll see."

"Well, I hope so. But, Barbara, the reason for my call is I'd like to list my house with you."

"So soon? Are you sure?" she asks.

"Yes, I'm sure."

"Well, then, of course, I can sell your house without any problem. Homes like yours are in great demand. You're still on Indigo Path in the Bayberry development, correct?"

"Yes, that's right. When do you think you can come over and take some photos?" I ask.

"That's up to you. I can come tonight if you'd like."

I look around the house and realize it's been far too long since I've really cleaned. I decide I'd better do some deep cleaning before I invite Barbara over. "How about tomorrow morning, say around nine?" I suggest.

"Okay, that will work. I'll see you then," Barbara says

and hangs up the phone.

After I clean the house, I sit down and call my mother. Wellington is the one part of my plan that I haven't figured out yet, but I'm thinking with a little coaxing, Mom might take him. I could tell her that he reminds me too much of Spencer and how much it hurts me to have him around. That could work. And, of course, I'm selling the house now and the "new apartment" I have yet to find most likely will not allow pets.

"Hello?"

"Hi, Mom, it's Adele."

"Oh, hi, honey. I was just thinking about you. Is everything okay?" Mom says in the concerned tone she always uses with me now. Ever since Spencer died, she has been worried about me; probably for good reason.

"Yes, Mom, everything is fine, except, well, I have one concern."

"What is it?" I could feel Mom's anticipation of pending doom on the other end of the phone.

"Well, it's not a big deal. At least I hope it won't be but it's about Wellington."

"Oh, Adele, please don't tell me Wellington has died...."

Yep. Just like I thought, she's expecting the worst. "No, Mom, it's nothing like that, but I do need to give him up."

"Why? Is there something wrong with him?"

"No, it's just that, well, he reminds me of Spencer....."

"Oh, Adele...." Her voice trails off, delicately.

"And, Mom, there's more. I've decided to sell the house."

An awful, massive silence suddenly exists between us. Mom is a firm believer in women owning their own homes and she knows that I know this. After Dad died five years ago, Lonnie and I suggested that Mom sell their house in Baldwinsville, but she insisted on staying put, stating that a woman who doesn't own property is destined for poverty, sounding like a suffragette. "A bit extreme, don't you think, Mom?" I had asked her with a smirk. She wasn't amused.

"Mom?"

"Yes, I'm still here. But you know how I feel about this, Adele. It's a mistake, and where will you live?"

"I'm hoping to find an upscale apartment in Armory Square, closer to the boutique." It's not a total lie, I have always dreamed about living downtown.

"So how much do you hope to earn off the sale of your house? It is in your name, right?" Mom knows the answer to her second question but she can't help asking me again. When Lonnie and I were first married thirteen years ago his credit was a disaster so it made better sense to put everything in my name; the cars, the house, the credit cards, everything, all in my name.

"Yes, the house is in my name but I'm not sure what I'll make on the sale. Barbara is coming over tomorrow morning to take pictures and list it. I'll know more then but I'm hoping to make at least fifty thousand dollars."

"Oh, I see," Mom says with an air of subdued exhilaration. "Hopefully, you'll make out well."

"I should. We've owned it for ten years," I say, not prepared for Mom's comeback.

"You mean *you've* owned it," Mom corrects me.

"Yes, Mom, *I've* owned it, for ten years." I say and wait for the air to clear between us before I press on. "So, Mom, about Wellington. Do you think you could take him?"

Her high voice suddenly erupts with laughter. "Sure, I'll take the old coot. Right after you sell the house, that is."

"Thanks, Mom, I love you."

"I love you, too, Adele," she says and hangs up the phone.

After powering down my cell phone for the night, I grab my bag off of the kitchen counter and dig around inside until I find the note from Carl. I read what it says as the cocktail napkin slips through my fingers and then wags in the air like a lost kite:

> *In case of reasonable regret, no hard feelings.*
> *Call me: 315-555-7568.*
> *Either way, I keep the money.*

4.

The next morning the air is full of summer sounds as Barbara Evans steps out of her Lexus and approaches my front door. Remnants of mist hang over the grass as she makes her way up the brick path carrying a bouquet of white flowers and a camera in both hands. One of my better life decisions was to have Orlando Ramos, my salesman, open the boutique for me every morning. Originally, it had become necessary when Spencer was hospitalized and, of course, after he died and I wasn't able to get out of bed for two weeks. But today it's just plain helpful; allowing me the time I need to meet with Barbara to discuss the sale of my home.

"Good morning, Barbara," I say as I open the front door and apply my standard smile. "Are these for me?"

"Yes, of course," she says as she hands me the flowers and steps inside. Barbara looks around the house with her trained, keen eye while I savor the moment. "The house looks beautiful!" she says, and, "let's put these flowers in a vase and set them on the dining room table for our first shot."

After all of the customary pictures of my four-bedroom colonial are taken, we each take a seat at the kitchen table. Barbara places some printouts of similar houses in Bayberry that have recently sold on the table before she begins. "I do believe we can list the house well above the comps you see here."

I pick up a couple of the printouts and scrutinize each house. "I agree," I say. "Some of these don't even have two bathrooms."

"Exactly," Barbara says. "And you have granite counter tops and updated appliances in your kitchen."

"So what do you think we should list it for?" I ask, anxiously.

"I think $185,000 is a good number. How do you feel about that price?"

My lips begin to twitch with amusement. I bought the house for $95,000 and I owe about $75,000 so this means I stand to walk away with approximately $100,000. Money that I intend to spread between Upstate Children's Hospital of Syracuse and my mother. "That sounds wonderful," I say.

"Great, then shall I list it for you today?" Barbara asks with an eager, almost greedy look on her face.

"Yes, please. How long do you think it will take to sell?" I ask, suddenly embarrassed by my naïve question.

"Well, I don't have a crystal ball but I would be surprised if it lasts on the market for more than thirty days," Barbara says with a hint of whimsy. "But, if we don't get any bites after the first week, we'll have an Open House, okay?"

"Sounds like a plan," I say as a genuine smile graces my face.

After I see Barbara to the door, I fill my travel cup with black coffee, pet Wellington behind his ears and wish him a good day, and walk outside and get into my car.

A Bit of Silver is located in Armory Square in downtown Syracuse; about a twenty minute drive from my home. After a few minutes on some local roads, I pull onto the interstate and head towards the city. As I increase my speed, the rhythmic sound of rubber meeting asphalt penetrates my ears and I am once again reminded of Spencer. Typically, on Saturday mornings, or after a terrible gray day of chemo, he would ride into work with me. I would show him my latest project and he would marvel at my collection of semi-precious stones and rocks while listening to Orlando's cheerful chatter and endless knock-knock jokes. The last time Spencer was strong enough to come into work with me, I was crafting a dragonfly pin for one of my customers in Rochester. I tried to keep things light by explaining to him as I worked how the wings were to be formed and the head attached. But when I turned around to see if he was listening, I saw tears of defeat blinding his eyes so I dropped my soldering iron and ran to his side. Spencer had met his Waterloo that day; he died three weeks later. I never could bring myself to finish the dragonfly pin.

I see the sign ahead for my exit and, as always, I think once again about driving into oncoming traffic and just ending the misery I call my life, but I can't. I have to stick to the plan, and I have until Labor Day to work out all of the details, I remind myself. For now, I will play the part of a happy Adele, getting on with her life.

As I enter the boutique, Orlando greets me with a kiss on the cheek. Rapt and radiant, he is dressed in a pair of turquoise blue skinny jeans and a black silk shirt that emphasize every corner and angle of his thin figure. A complex man with exquisite taste in jewelry, he is an extraordinarily competent salesman, and the customers love him specifically for his overt sexuality. With a dark green glint of his eyes and his endearing smile, he asks, "Are you okay Deli?" (Only Orlando calls me Deli.)

I first met Orlando three years ago on a puddle jumper from Syracuse to Philadelphia. I was on my way to visit my friend, Deirdre, who had just delivered her third child but Orlando was flying back home to Manayunk, a suburb of Philadelphia, for a much more somber occasion. He needed to bury his mother. On our shared sojourn south, I quickly learned that Orlando adored his "Moms", as he called her, but was in no shape for the flight home. When I took my seat next him – me in the aisle, he next to the window – he immediately apologized in advance for all the blubbering he intended to do. But before long, we were talking about the latest fashions coming out of New York and Paris, and my signature silver hair pin, which he admired greatly and wanted to buy. I suspected he wanted it for his Moms, to bury her with, but when he admitted he would keep it and wear it himself, we both erupted with laughter. Before we touched down in Philly, Orlando learned that I owned a Bit of Silver in Syracuse, his newly adopted city, and asked me if I happened to be in the market for a remarkably talented salesperson. As it turned out, I was, so I hired him right on the spot, and have never looked back.

"Yes, I'm fine, Orlando," I say as I step behind the jewelry case and quickly survey our inventory. "I met with my realtor this morning is all."

"Oh?" Orlando asks with the rise of one well-manicured brow.

"I've decided to sell my house."

"Oh, Deli, that is great news!" he cackles. "Will you finally get an apartment downtown close to me? Pretty please, pretty please!"

I can almost hear the saliva gurgling in his cheeks. "Yes, that's my plan, Orlando," I say with a small secret smile, just as our first customer of the day, a man with flawless features, enters the shop.

"I'll take this one," Orlando says blushing with delight as he greets the handsome man with his award-winning smile.

As Orlando tends to our new customer, I fire up the

computer and wait for it to respond. I flip the day-at-a-glance calendar on my desk to Friday, June 14, and count the money in the cash register. The computer is still warming up when I glance in the direction of the new customer and find our gazes locked in mutual surprise. Unspoken words lay deep inside his eyes. Captivated, I decide to introduce myself. I am, after all, the proprietor of this shop. It is only fitting that I make myself available to him. Driven by an obscure impulse, I walk over to where he and Orlando are now examining some silver bangles and extend my hand outward. "Hello, my name is Adele Hamilton," I say and his face radiates with goodwill as if a candle has suddenly been lit.

He shakes my hand. His hand is warm but it is the bright alertness of his gaze that sees right through me. I stare bashfully at him for a solid minute until I hear Orlando clear his throat, bringing me back down to earth with a start. Finally, the man speaks, his velvet-blue eyes focused entirely on me. "Hi, I've heard about your fantastic jewelry. That's why I stopped in. My name is Morgan. Morgan Spencer."

My smile, once triumphant and graceful, disappears as I try to catch my breath. Just the sound of Spencer's name launches me into a mild panic attack. I look at Orlando who understands, instinctively, and takes over the conversation. I feel my face going all the wrong sort of shape as I try to fake another smile but I fear I look weak-chinned and feeble. Eventually I manage to speak and add to their ongoing conversation. "Well, that's wonderful. Are you looking for something in particular?"

Morgan Spencer looks around the store and steps lightly along the hardwood floors. His chestnut brown hair is threaded with a touch of silver and his straight, perfect nose rests prominently on his oval face. Then in the calm space, like an old friendship, he asks, "Do you have any dragonflies?"

Once again, I need some time to regain my composure while Orlando, who always has my back, keeps Morgan engaged in a titillating conversation about jewelry shaped like insects as I do my best to maintain a stiff upper lip. Finally, Orlando turns to me and reiterates Morgan's question, "Deli, do you think we can make some type of dragonfly piece for Mr. Spencer?"

"Wow, please just call me Morgan," he says, and Orlando smiles.

I pull my professional smile out of my hip pocket and slap it across my face. "Why, yes, certainly," I say. "What did you have in mind, a pin perhaps?"

His eyes sparkle with a million small fires as he holds his gaze on me. "Well, I'm not exactly sure," he says. "It's a gift for my niece, Waverly, who is graduating from middle school next week. She has a thing for dragonflies."

"In that case," I say. "I would suggest either a bracelet or a necklace. When do you need it by?"

"Her graduation ceremony is a week from tomorrow, is that too soon?" He asks with a gleaming white smile accented by delicious dimples.

I know that I can make a bracelet or a charm for a necklace in a couple of days, but I pause before I answer. "I think that is possible. Which are you thinking, a bracelet or a charm?"

Morgan tips his head and smiles at me once again. I feel a slight flutter in my stomach. "I'll leave that up to you. Whatever you think will work." Then he reaches into his back pocket and pulls out his business card. "Here is my card. Please call me when it's ready, and I will swing by and pick it up."

"We haven't discussed the price yet," I say.

"Please just design something you feel would be appropriate for a teenage girl and I will pay for it," he says with an air of confidence.

"Okay then," I say. "I'll call you in about a week to pick it up."

"Do you need a deposit?" He asks.

"No, that's not necessary. If for some reason you change your mind, we will put it in our display case and someone will eventually buy it," I say, confidently.

"I won't change my mind," he says as he smiles once again and walks out the door and onto the street. Shamelessly, Orlando and I both watch him as he walks away.

"It's always the same old story," Orlando says with a feeble pout. "The good ones are always straight."

I smile and look down at Morgan's card. "He owns an auto body shop called *CarFIX*, right here in Syracuse."

"Too bad I don't own a car," Orlando jokes as we get back to work.

5.

I wake early the next morning. Barbara has already arranged for our first showing today and I need to get downtown to the boutique to begin work on the new piece for Morgan Spencer's niece. It took a lot of soul searching, after I arrived home last night, but I have managed to set aside the coincidence regarding the dragonfly pin and how much that initially bothered me. I have decided I'm going to make a delicate silver bracelet of a dragonfly with overlapping wings that will lie on the wrist like a bow with a simple chain connecting it in the back. I have always had the ability to see these images in my mind and then transfer them quickly into a sketch for the customer; a skill I honed at Alfred University. Today I will show my sketch to Orlando. If he likes it, I'm golden.

When I walk into the kitchen, the sun splashes through the large picture window where I find Wellington lying on the floor sunning his fluffy body. "Come on, big guy, let's get you some breakfast," I say as I fill his dish. Wellington ignores me.

I press the button on my Keurig and wait for my coffee to brew while I look through a pile of bills. Although I'm going to make out on the sale of the house, big time, Lonnie did leave me alone with all of these household bills so I figure we are even. Setting the bills aside, I think about Morgan Spencer as the irresistible aroma of fresh coffee wafts up to my nose. I take a sip from my travel mug and let it roll around on my tongue as I wonder whether or not Morgan drinks coffee and, if so, what kind? *Rich and robust or mild and artificially flavored?* It isn't until I get to my car that I realize I've been daydreaming for five full minutes about the coffee habits of a total stranger. I begin to smile and decide right on the spot that I need to get laid at least once before I die. Ten weeks until Labor Day, I think, as I pull out of the driveway and insert a CD into the stereo.

The Plain White T's soon infuse my body with light indie rock and, like everything, they remind me of Spencer. We saw them together, last summer, at the New York State Fair where they put on a light show; white heat encompassing nothing and everything all at once. Spencer loved them. He sang along to all of their songs to which he knew all of the words. I bought him a CD and a tee-shirt as we exited the fairgrounds and we laughed for days about the shirt being a "plain white t." Listening to the CD now is simply too painful for me so I turn off the stereo and tuck the CD beneath the front seat and drive the rest of the way to work in silence.

As I pull into Armory Square, Syracuse University students appropriately attired in oranges and blues march through the streets carrying signs in complete solidarity. What they are protesting against, or for, this week is beyond me. I quickly park my Civic and cut across the square and enter the boutique where I find Orlando already inside.

"What is it this week?" I ask as I set my cup down on the counter and tuck my bag underneath the desk.

"Racial diversity," Orlando answers without looking up, engrossed as he is in a computer spreadsheet.

"That's refreshing," I say referring to last month's brouhaha over the alleged poor quality of the food in the school cafeteria. "Good for them."

"Yes. Deli, I was looking over our purchase orders for the month and I don't see an order for silver. Our inventory is getting dangerously low."

Hampered by the undeniable fact that he is right, time suddenly slows to a nauseating crawl as I try to think of something to say. I give a pregnant pause before finally filling up the space between us with a lie. "That can't be right. Are you sure?"

"Yes, I've checked it three times."

"Wow, that's weird," I say as I look over his shoulder and pretend to study the screen. "I'm glad you found it. I'll place an order first thing Monday morning."

"Great," Orlando says, satisfied with my response. "So what's on the hit parade today?"

"Well," I say. "I'm going to begin work on the bracelet for Morgan Spencer. But first, my dear, I need you to take a look at my sketch." I pull out my drawing pad from the canvas bag draped over my shoulder and turn the pages until I find the dragonfly.

Orlando holds the sketch pad up to the light next to the window and carefully scrutinizes my drawing for several minutes. Finally he turns to me and says, "Deli, this is beautiful."

"So you like it?"

"Like it? I adore it! I think it may be one of your best designs. You should really think about making several of these. I'm sure they'd sell," he says as he hands me back my sketch pad.

"Okay, maybe I will. Thanks, Orlando."

With the lingering fresh scent of coffee still in my nostrils and the high praise from Orlando, I head back to the workshop and begin selecting the materials I need to form the dragonfly bracelet.

My interest in anything art related was formed when I was a small child and my mother would let me color on the walls in my bedroom. She was like that; a free spirit, and I loved her for it. In fact, Mom did all sorts of cool art projects with me like this. We made crazy little creatures together out of homemade salt dough and finger painted them outside on the back porch on large sheets of parchment paper that Dad would bring home from the printing shop where he worked. But it wasn't until after I got to Alfred University that I discovered my true love, jewelry making. I have always been able to sketch just about anything, but turning a sketch into something tangible thrilled me, and I knew instantly, in my first year of college, that I had to do this for a living.

As I forge and bend the metal into shape for the bracelet, I think about Orlando and what will happen to him after I'm gone. Something I didn't think about until he asked me about the missing silver order this morning. Initially, I had just planned to close the shop and assumed Orlando would find employment elsewhere. But now, as I think about it more, I realize that Orlando would be devastated and may not be able to find work in Syracuse for months. Besides, he could manage the store; it's just that he doesn't know anything about making jewelry.

As I carve the delicate pattern into the wings, I remember my old Alma Mater again and their internship program. If I could hire a recent grad and work with them every day until Labor Day. Well, then, maybe after I'm gone the two of them could keep a Bit of Silver open. I would like that. I love this boutique, just not enough to hang onto life without Spencer.

As I set the bracelet to the side to cool down, I decide to talk to Orlando about becoming an equal partner in a Bit of Silver. And there is no time like the present.

As I re-enter the showroom, I find it vibrating with the presence of many shoppers eager to make their purchases. I overhear a familiar voice rippling with a seductive tone followed by the sudden bellow of laughter and cheery chatter from Orlando.

When he turns around I don't recognize him at first, dressed in his skin-tight bicycle riding gear. He now has a boyish quality much different than the man I met yesterday. But it is undeniably him. Morgan Spencer has returned. "Adele," he says with a wide smile.

I begin to blink stupidly as I try not to stare directly at his well-proportioned body or his dark brown hair streaming wildly behind his ears or his cheeks tinted passion-red. *Jesus, he looks like a super model standing in front of a wind machine ready for his close-up.* "Morgan, what a surprise. I thought we wouldn't see you for another week," I say as I remove my work apron from around my waist and shake his hand.

"I was just cycling around Onondaga Lake. I thought I'd stop by and see how you were doing."

"Funny you should mention that, I was just working on your niece's bracelet," I say a little surprised by his need to check up on me so soon.

"Oh, I didn't mean how the piece was coming along. I'm sure you will have that finished in time. I was just wondering if you would like to join me for a cup of coffee sometime."

He is strongly erotic standing before me in his navy blue and green cycling suit and I am completely smitten. Even though I don't feel like going out on a date, I decide I need a break from my routine. Besides, I'll be dead soon and none of this will matter. "Yes, that would be nice," I say a little too quickly as I look across the room at Orlando who is pretending to faint.

"Fantastic. How about tomorrow for brunch?"

"That would be nice," I say.

"Perfect, I'll pick you up here at ten," he says as he reaches for his helmet resting on the counter. His arm accidentally brushes up against mine and it feels like a thousand bolts of electricity running wildly through my body, and I tremble inside like a silly school girl.

"Okay," is all I can think to say as he smiles and leaves the boutique.

Afterwards, I find Orlando finishing up a sale with a customer who has just bought an expensive Larimar stone ring. "Orlando, when you have a minute come back into the shop."

"Sure, Deli, I'll be right there."

Cozy in my lair, I pick up the dragonfly bracelet and continue working. I suddenly realize that I am smiling as I think about my morning curiosity regarding Morgan's coffee habits. I then wonder what I'll wear to brunch tomorrow, as if it matters. Ten minutes later Orlando joins me faking a whimper. "So I heard that you and Mr. Lovely have a date tomorrow."

My laugh is sudden and foreign. "Yes, it appears to be so."

"Good for you, Deli, it's time," Orlando says as he puts his arms around me and then leans over and looks at the bracelet. "Oh, Deli, this is coming along very nicely. Great job."

"Thanks, Orlando," I say, especially grateful for the hug.

"I still think you should make as many of them as you can. They'll sell like discontinued eye liner at a drag queen convention." Tickled, by Orlando's powers of persuasion, I laugh once again and agree to make more bracelets.

"Orlando, I want to talk to you about something. Let's

take a seat."

"Oh, dear, this sounds serious. Should I get some tissues?"

"Maybe," I say as I take a seat on one of the two stools in the shop. I clear my throat before I speak. "Orlando, you've been a loyal partner and confidant of mine ever since I opened the boutique seven years ago."

Orlando nods his head in agreement.

"Well, I've been thinking, and if you are interested, I think it's high time I make you an equal partner of a Bit of Silver."

Orlando squeals with delight. "I was right, I do need those tissues," he says as he reaches for a box nearby and dries his eyes. "Deli, this is wonderful. I've always dreamed about becoming co-owner. Wow! I don't know what to say."

"Say, 'yes', dummy," I say with a loving smile.

"Yes, of course, yes!" Orlando says as he pulls me from my stool and gives me a big hug. He then drops his arms and rests them on his slim hips and declares, "And I *must* get me some new business cards!"

"Good idea," I say. "And on Monday I'll contact our attorney and have the paperwork drawn up."

"Ah, who is *our* attorney?" Orlando asks in a hushed tone.

I laugh once again and tell him I will explain everything he needs to know on Monday.

6.

Last night I had a terrifying dream that I was walking in unfamiliar woods and could hear Spencer's voice calling out for me. But it was so dark I could not see him, so I stumbled about, following the sound of his voice. First it was coming from my left, behind a tree, and then off to the right in the distance and then somewhere behind me. His voice began to drown out in the dense evening mist. As I turned in circles and struggled to find him again, a wolf suddenly appeared and began to speak. "Spencer is dead and you will never see him again, Adele." Its eyes were black and familiar, but dead like black beans. Before I could respond, the wolf morphed into Carl from the Lounge who then had the eyes of a wolf, gold and piercing. Carl threw back his head and began to howl as I screamed, "Spencer! Spencer! Spencer!"

I rise, a bit groggy, from my bed, but instead of trying to get more sleep, I sit up and turn on the television. Sleep has been eluding me for weeks. The local weatherman broadcasts from outside the station's studio deck in downtown Syracuse. A salmon-pink sky is his backdrop. He forecasts some early morning showers that he promises should clear up by 10:00 a.m. "Then nothing but bright yellow sunshine for the rest of the day with a high of 72 degrees," he says with his trademark smile. *Perfect*, I think, as I get out of bed and step into the shower.

After I shower, I step into my closet and begin the search for the perfect first date outfit. After several frustrating minutes, filled with regret over not shopping for myself in months, I settle on a flirty pale bluish-green cotton dress that is open at the waste in the back and falls a few inches above my knees. With it, I select a pair of well-worn leather gladiator sandals and slip them onto my feet. I wear my hair long and straight with the exception of the carefully-placed silver flower pin that tucks my blond hair neatly behind my left ear.

In the kitchen I make myself a cup of coffee and decide to listen to some soft music for a little while. I like the old stuff Mom listens to; Van Morrison, Dylan and The Allman Brothers so I click on my Pandora shuffle on my computer and turn up the volume good and loud. *Wish You Were Here* by Pink Floyd bellows out and I can't stand it. Everything reminds me of Spencer. I turn off the music, walk out front and take a seat on the front porch.

Just as I get comfortable, a cool breeze blows in soft and low as the sky turns dark and the sun retreats behind a large storm cloud. The leaves on the trees make an upward turn with a gentle, mesmerizing sway. The dampness sets in quickly as a welcomed mist until it runs boldly across the road and bleeds up onto the porch. The dogs in the neighborhood howl, my heart jumps and the thunder rolls, threatening me with each and every roar. "Let it take me, let it roll," I whisper as tears stream down my face. Suddenly I regret my decision to have brunch with Morgan and think about calling it off.

I look past the porch and watch as the puddles on the street grow wider. I am reminded once again of how Spencer and his friends would love to wade in them after a summer rain. I dry my tears with the back of my hand and decide to keep my date with Morgan. If nothing else, I could use a drink and drinking alone has become pathetic, even for me.

At 9:30 I decide to head downtown. I lock up the house and take my normal route into the city. When I arrive in

Armory Square, I park in my typical spot and wait a few minutes before getting out of the car. As predicted, the rain has stopped and it is a beautiful Central New York morning. Bright pink and red rhododendrons are huddled in the cleft of every hollow along the shops that line the streets of the square and the lazy rays of the sun beat down through my windshield warming my cheeks.

As I step out of my car and walk to a Bit of Silver, where I am to meet Morgan, I turn the corner and see him waiting for me. He is dressed in a pair of dark blue designer jeans and a gray tee-shirt with the brand name *Diesel* written across the front of it in a mustard color. I smile as I watch him bend over at the waist and brush some mud from his dark gray boat shoes. When I approach the boutique, he is the first to speak. "Good morning, Adele, you look beautiful," he says as he boldly gives me a peck on the cheek.

"Thank you," I say as I try not to blush and return his smile. "Where are we going?" I ask.

"I thought we would try LoFo's," he says. "Does that sound okay to you?"

"Yes, as a matter of fact my business partner, Orlando, has recommended it to me several times but I have yet to try it," I say.

"Well, then, let's go," Morgan says as he extends his bended arm and leads the way.

A street café, LoFo's has eight tables draped in white table cloths that are separated from the bustle of customers waiting to get a seat with gold stanchions and black velour rope. Bare yellow light bulbs strung on wires crisscross the many trees above us. Luckily, Morgan has called ahead so we walk right in and are seated next to a large sugar maple tree. We gaze bashfully at one another for a while until our waitress arrives. Morgan orders the Cajun egg sandwich and I get the French toast with stewed pears. Over brunch, Morgan explains that he first opened his auto body shop ten years ago after his wife, Gloria, had died. Prior to that he worked for a local shop but made more money doing side jobs restoring old cars and motorcycle tanks so he figured, why not branch out on his own? So he did. He has lived in Central New York his entire life even though he had been born in Virginia.

"What brought your family to New York?" I ask as I bite into a piece of French toast.

"My dad got a job he couldn't refuse, at Lockheed Martin as an engineer," he explains as he wipes his mouth.

"What about you?"

"I'm an only child, born and raised in the Syracuse area," I confess. "After college I married my high school sweetheart, Lonnie. We had a son together; I opened a Bit of Silver, on my own, and then Lonnie and I split up about two months ago."

"What's your son's name?" Morgan asks, innocently.

I ignore the dull rumbling in the hollow of my gut and quietly say, "Spencer."

"You're kidding me!" Morgan says with a hardy roar. "What a coincidence."

"Yes, I know," I say as I take a sip of my mimosa.

"How old is Spencer now?" Morgan asks as he takes another bite of his sandwich and looks down at his plate.

I stare out the window and wish I could take back the day as I set down my fork. I shouldn't have come here, I just knew it. The whole idea of going out on a date when I'm simultaneously planning my own death is crazy but I answer his question. "Spencer died of Leukemia eight months ago."

Morgan's shifts uncomfortably in his seat. "Oh, Adele, I'm so sorry for your loss. I had no idea."

"No, of course you didn't, that's okay," I say. "I need to get used to being able to talk about it. Really, it's okay," I say as I reach my hand across the table and rest it on top of the table next to his.

"How about we get out of here?" he asks. "I'd like to take you sailing, if you are up for it."

He has somehow read my mind. *Why not go sailing?* My life will be over soon, I remind myself, and none of this will matter. "Sailing, really?" I ask. "Am I dressed for that?"

"Yes, of course, let's go," Morgan waves to the waitress and asks for our check. After he drops two twenty dollar bills on the table, we get up and leave the restaurant.

We walk to the parking lot together and discover that Morgan is parked three spots over from me. He drives a Subaru Impreza, which he has painted flat black and added some tricked-out rims to. On top is a bike rack holding his silver and white bike. "Would you prefer to follow me or should I drive us to the lake together?" Morgan asks.

"I'll ride with you," I say, throwing caution to the wind as I jump into his car. Nothing matters to me anymore, and I am even more adventurous than usual. Knowing that you will soon be dead has its perks.

Ten minutes later we arrive at the Onondaga Yacht Club in Liverpool. As we walk across the lot to his sailboat, Morgan explains to me that the yacht club is a sailing, motor and social club for its members and guests only. It is situated next to the scenic Onondaga Lake Trail where Morgan cycles and adjacent to the Onondaga County Marina. "What I like about the club the most is it's not snooty," he says.

"How so?" I ask, not completely convinced.

"Well, for one, OYC holds weekly handicap sailboat races and special holiday races."

"That sounds nice," I say.

"Yea, it is, but what I enjoy the most are the Sunday evening lakeside picnics and, of course, the sailing," he says as we arrive next to his boat, the *Summer Sled*.

"Nice name for a boat," I say. "What do you do in the winter?"

"Snowboard," he says with a bright twinkle in his eye. "What else?"

We walk out onto the dock and Morgan takes my hand and helps me aboard the *Summer Sled*. The twenty-five foot beauty rocks a little in the water as Morgan helps me to my seat. He then retrieves two bright yellow life jackets and a Syracuse Orange wind breaker from a small cupboard and wraps the wind breaker around my shoulders. "You don't have to put on the life jacket if you don't want to but we need to have them aboard with us," Morgan explains.

I decide to tough it out. *Maybe I'll drown and save the hit man a bullet.* I rest the life jacket next to my feet as Morgan casts off. He then jumps back into the boat and takes a seat next to me and starts the motor. Morgan skillfully steers us out into open water and after a few minutes, he asks me to take the tiller. "Hold her steady and point her into the wind," he says, and I think he's kidding but learn he is not when he leaves his seat and goes forward to "hoist the mainsail." I hold the tiller steady, as instructed, and pretend to know what it means to point her into the wind. The boat shudders slightly as the sails unfurl with a snap. Morgan then leans over my shoulder and cuts the engine. It becomes deadly quiet and we are sailing.

As my ears adjust to the stillness, I hear the lake

crashing against the bow and notice an unbroken emerald green forest at the shore line. I am reminded of last night's dream about the wolf but the smell of the warm wind coming off the lake is so invigorating that I close my eyes and lift my face to the sky. For a moment, I allow myself to forget about my Spencer. "This is beautiful," I say.

"First time sailing?" Morgan asks with a gentle smile.

"Yes," I admit.

"I thought so," Morgan says. "I can always spot a newbie. But I have to warn you, it can get under your skin if you let it, and then you won't be able to imagine a world without the sound of the sails and the sea."

"I can understand how that could happen to a person," I say as I rise from my seat and look over the side of the boat and into the syrupy current.

Morgan joins me and puts his arm around my shoulder. "Do you like it, Adele?"

I look up at him, half-delirious with pleasure as if suddenly stabbed by the miracle of the water, and say, "Yes, I love it."

7.

We sail for three hours until our faces are bronzed and my belly is famished.

When we finally return to shore, Morgan jumps out onto the dock, ties off the *Summer Sled* and then helps me to the dock. The bright afternoon sun continues to linger on our shoulders as we walk back to Morgan's car, and I suddenly find myself not wanting the day to end.

We stop in front of the yacht club and Morgan asks, "Would you like to stop in here and have a light bite to eat and maybe a drink before heading home?" He has read my mind again, but before I can answer he adds, "They make a killer Mojito with fresh mint leaves."

"Ummm, that sounds wonderful," I say as we turn around and head into the clubhouse.

Inside, a warm pool of light floods the cozy room from the bank of windows overlooking the lake. Morgan selects a table for us next to a west-facing window and pulls out my chair for me. I take a seat and gaze out at the lake that shimmers with pearl-like sparkle, mirroring the crystal blue sky above. Morgan takes his seat, opens his menu and then looks over the top of it and stares across the table at me.

"What?" I ask, quite surprised.

"If I didn't already tell you today, Adele, you look beautiful. Especially now, with that sun on your face, you look so full of life."

My whole being secretly seethes with shame as I think about my scheduled demise. I don't know how to respond to him as my mind has suddenly become empty, sober and joyless like a sheet of blank paper. But, instinctively, I manage to add, "thank you, Morgan. I'm having such a wonderful day."

The waitress arrives and smiles brightly at Morgan and gives me a slight nod. "Hi, Morgan, how are you?"

"Hi, Valerie, I'm doing great. I'd like you to meet my friend, Adele."

Valerie is about twenty-five-years old, brunette and has a very pretty face. She smiles at me, initially, but then follows it up with an odd, frosty look when she thinks I'm not looking. "Hello," she says.

"Nice to meet you, Valerie," I say and smile as widely as I can and return my gaze to Morgan who orders us two Mojitos. My womanly intuition tells me something is amiss with Valerie but it is none of my business so I let it go. "So what's good on the menu?" I ask maintaining a pleasant smile.

"Everything," Morgan says. "But I think I'm going to have an Angus burger with a side of steak fries."

"That's a light bite?" I tease.

"Okay, I lied, I'm starving!" he says. "There is something about the lake and the sun that makes me hungry as a bear." We laugh just as Valerie returns to our table with the Mojitos. She leans over the table a little too far and the slippery tray suddenly falls from her hands landing both icy drinks directly in my lap. The glasses and the tray crash to the floor, and Morgan jumps to his feet while I brush ice cubes and mint leaves from my dress.

A few of the other patrons in the clubhouse turn around in their seats to watch the scene unfolding at our table. The manager, an older gentleman wearing an unfortunate toupee, rushes over and begins to apologize profusely. "I'm so sorry, Mr. Spencer, miss," he says as he helps me wipe the drinks from my dress. "Naturally, we will pay for your dry cleaning."

"Oh, that's not necessary, really," I say. "Everyone makes mistakes."

"I'm so sorry," Valerie says as she bends down and begins picking up the pieces of broken glass, ice cubes and mint leaves from the floor. "Really I am. Can I get you two more drinks?"

Morgan looks at me and asks, "Do you want to leave?"

"No. Please bring us two more drinks," I say quietly to Valerie who is still on the floor.

"Absolutely!" The manager responds. "And, of course, Mr. Spencer, today's meal is on the house."

"That's not necessary, Daniel." Morgan says as he pulls out my chair again and takes his seat.

"I insist," the manager says as he walks away with a very embarrassed Valerie.

"Are you sure you're okay?" Morgan asks.

"Yes, I'm fine," I say. "It's going to take more than a little rum and some mint leaves to ruin this day."

When the drinks arrive for the second time, Valerie gingerly sets my drink down first and then Morgan's. "Thank you, Valerie," Morgan says and lifts his glass to mine. "To smooth sailing from here on out."

"Yes, sir," I say as we clink our glasses together and take a large sip of our drinks. Morgan is right, the drink is amazing.

We linger over our meal and talk for several more hours. I tell him about my split from Lonnie, and my shop and my decision to make Orlando a full partner. He explains his body shop and his deceased wife to me the best he can. We order coffee, but decline dessert.

Narrow strips of crimson appear in the western sky and catch my eye. I look down at my watch and am surprised to learn its 7:30 p.m. Across the lake, fringes of brilliant red and white sunlight gleams through the trees. "It looks like it's going to be a beautiful day tomorrow," I say.

"Red sky at night...," Morgan says with a smile as he gazes out across the lake.

"Spencer used to love that expression." My smile retreats from my face, and I take my last sip of black coffee. "I guess I should be going. Thank you for a lovely meal and a terrific day."

"You're welcome," Morgan says as he finishes up the last drop of his coffee and stands up.

As we walk from the restaurant, Valerie stops us in the parking lot and once again apologizes for spilling the drinks in my lap. I assure her it's no big deal and wish her a good night. When we get to Morgan's car, he looks down at his feet and for the first time since I've known him he looks uncomfortable in his own skin. "Adele, I'm really sorry about tonight. Valerie spilling the drinks on you I mean."

"What do you mean? That's not your fault. Don't be silly," I say.

Morgan's face is twisted and suddenly sad. "Well, it might have been. Valerie and I dated for a little while, but it just wasn't right and…"

"Morgan, please stop. That's none of my business," I say.

A thin mist hangs across the lake and the pink-and-gold sky above glows brightly when he leans over and begins kissing me. His fleshy lips are warm against mine and my body tingles from head to toe. Birds clatter in the space between the nearby trees and I am shocked to learn that I never want to stop kissing him. *What is wrong with me?*

8.

    Altered, I arrive downtown early on the following Monday morning to open the boutique. I walk across Armory Square and into a brilliant green and cool summer day and smile at the big sphere of pink blossoms in the window boxes outside the boutique which look like bridesmaids' bouquets. No matter how depressed I have become, I will always love the smell of flowers.

    As I turn the key in the lock, I am reminded that I have a busy day today. I need to contact my old professor, Ryan Carmichael, and ask about the internship program at Alfred U. Contact my attorney, Claire, and ask her to draw up the paperwork necessary to form a Limited Partnership with Orlando, and then show Orlando how to purchase raw materials for the shop.

    Once inside, I stand alone in the still and perfect quietness of my humble surroundings. The walls are painted a cool silvery-gray which look fantastically regal against the natural warm tones of the yellow hardwood floors. The lights are low but the polished jewelry, a mass of whirling shapes, sparkles brightly inside the glass showcases while the raw smell of metallic silver emanates from my workshop and tickles my nose. I take it all in when a sensation of startling sweetness settles into my soul. In the space of a heartbeat, I realize how much I am going to miss a Bit of Silver. I brush it off, set down my bag and turn on the overhead lights and the music system just as the tiny brass bell above the front door jingles marking Orlando's arrival.

    "Good morning, partner," Orlando says and gives me a

kiss on the cheek. He places his backpack on the counter behind the front desk and takes a seat at the stool beside me. "So, dish it out. How was your date?"

Orlando looks at me with eyes that dance while I recant all of the intimate details of my date with Morgan. He laughs when I tell him about Valerie spilling the drinks on me and adds, "Ah huh, that was on purpose, girlfriend," when I mention that she and Morgan used to date. "So are you going out with him again?"

"I don't know, he didn't mention anything," I say as I turn on the computer. "But, enough about that, I'm going to call our attorney now and ask her to start work on the paperwork for our partnership."

"Great," Orlando says. "And we need to order more silver today, too."

"Yes, and I want to show you how to do that, okay?"

"You got it," Orlando says in his cheerful, friendly voice.

"One other thing, Orlando, I'm thinking about hiring an intern; hopefully a recent grad from Alfred that I can train to make our style of jewelry."

"Oh?" Orlando asks. "Why is that?"

"Well, I've been thinking, I would like to take some time off, maybe beginning around Labor Day and it would be nice to have a second jewelry maker. I'm certain we can afford a modest salary so what do you think?"

"I think if you think it's a good idea than let's go for it," Orlando says.

"All right, I'll make some calls this morning and hopefully we'll have some candidates to look at within a week or two. Of course, I'll want you to help with the interviews."

"Sounds good," Orlando says as a small flock of

college girls enter the store.

After all of my calls have been made and the silver order placed, I return to the workshop and finish work on Morgan's bracelet. I have to admit it, it is breathtakingly beautiful and so very dainty I am certain any middle school girl would love it. I walk out into the showroom to show it to Orlando when my cell phone begins to ring. At first I don't recognize the number but then remember it is my Aunt Sue, my mother's sister, who lives next door to Mom.

"Hello, Aunt Sue?" I ask.

"Yes, Adele, it's me," she says with a whispery rasp. Aunt Sue has been a smoker all her life. She is ten years older than Mom and also a widow. The only reason I can figure the two sisters have not moved in together is because of the same stubborn resolve they both share that says they *must* own their own home.

"Well what a surprise, Aunt Sue, what's up?" I ask.

With a whimpering, hysterical note in her voice Aunt Sue says, "Adele, honey, your mom has had a stroke. She's at Upstate Medical."

There is a long pause as I try to comprehend what she has just told me. Mom is in great health. She exercises regularly and eats right, doesn't drink or smoke. This doesn't make sense. "When? How?" I ask in a panic.

"This morning," Aunt Sue explains. "I was with her, thank God, when it happened. We were having our coffee when she suddenly became confused and was unable to talk. The right side of her face went numb and looked as if it were sliding off. Naturally, I knew something was wrong."

"Oh my God," I say. "Did the paramedics come?"

"Yes, they got here ten minutes after I called them."

"Can I see her?" I ask as Orlando becomes aware of my rigid body language.

"Yes, she's in intensive care, where I'm calling you from now."

"All right, thank you, Aunt Sue. I'll be right there," I say as I close my phone.

When I arrive at Upstate it is bustling with activity and I am reminded of Spencer, who was the last person I came to visit in a hospital. I enter the bay where my mother lies still. "She is asleep now," the nurse explains as I sit next to her bed in the dead, cold, empty silence of the room. I watch the heart monitor for movement to validate her existence when the automatic blood pressure cuff begins to babble and cluck and registers her numbers, 120/70.

I sit back and look at the white tiles on the ceiling when I hear Mom's weak voice. "Adele?"

I stand up and lean over her bed. "Yes, Mom, it's me" I say as I take her hand in mine. "I'm here."

In a soft sibilant sound she whispers one last time before falling back to sleep, "Thank you for coming, sweetheart, I don't know what I would do without you."

9.

It's 2:18 a.m. I should be asleep but I have become a night creature, same as Wellington. I walk into the kitchen for a cup of chamomile and peer out the window and into the back yard. The moon has cast its radiance over the dense evening mist like a fuzzy blue blanket and twilight reigns. Soft night murmurs have become my companions. Crickets chirp and a lonesome train whistles in the distance as I realize I am even more depressed now than I was when I first met Carl. The doctors say that Mom will recover, but she will need help. Luckily, Aunt Sue is right next door, but I know Mom wants my help. I will do my best, I tell myself, and hopefully by Labor Day she will be stronger and able to manage without me. I think about Orlando and wonder if he can learn all there is to know about running a Bit of Silver in time. Lastly, I think about Morgan and wonder if I should ever see him again.

I pull my phone out of my bag and see that I have received a text message from Orlando. Apparently Morgan has sent a potted mint plant wrapped in a silver bow to the boutique for me with a note that reads, *Smooth sailing from here on out, call me when you can, Morgan.* Orlando, a true romantic, thought it was a wonderfully unique gesture and added, "So, are you going to call him?"

"What do you think, Wellington, should I call him?" I ask as the cat stands at my feet looking up at me with a queer look on his round, sweet face. Wellington tries to answer me with a strange, drawn out *meoooow.* The tea kettle is ready so I pour some hot water over the tea bag in my cup and take a seat at the table. I take a sip of the herbal tea when I hear the distinctive clicking of my cell phone. *Would the nurses at the hospital be texting me?*

I am surprised to see it's from him.

Morgan: I know you won't get this until daybreak but I'm awake now and thought I'd send you a text. Thinking of you.

I decide to go ahead and text him back.

Me: Hi, I'm awake too. Thank you for the mint plant.

Morgan: Wow! What a surprise, why are you up so late?

Me: Rough day, my mom suffered a stroke today. I can't sleep.

Morgan: I'm so sorry to hear that, is she going to be okay?

Me: Yes, she's at Upstate Medical. I visited with her the entire afternoon.

Morgan: Would you like company?

Me: Now?

Morgan: Sure, why not? I can bring a movie for us to watch.

And then the bad girl in me decides, sure, why not so I type: OK, I'm at 16 Indigo Path in Liverpool.

Morgan: See you in 15.

I abandon my cup of tea and jump into the shower and quickly shave my legs and then slip into a pink jogging suit and flip flops. I douse myself with my favorite perfume and put on some lip gloss but no other make-up. Dead soon or not, I want to have sex at least once more before I die. When I re-enter the kitchen I hear Morgan's car pull up out front. "You be nice," I say to Wellington as I open the front door and welcome Morgan inside. He is carrying a bottle of white wine, my favorite, and a movie, *Silver Linings Playbook*.

He gives me a kiss hello, which I return, briefly, and then take the bottle of wine into the kitchen and pour us each a glass. Meanwhile, Morgan looks around the house, and I can feel a compliment coming. "This place is beautiful," he says. "I saw the 'For Sale' sign on the front lawn. You're selling?"

"Yes," I say as I hand him a glass of wine. "Now with Lonnie and Spencer gone it doesn't make sense for me to own such a big house."

"Where will you live?" Morgan asks as he samples the wine.

"Probably somewhere downtown, near the boutique," I lie as I take a sip. "This is delicious, thank you."

"I'm glad you like it. It's from a Finger Lakes winery, Lamoreaux Landing, in Ovid. We should go there sometime," he adds.

"Maybe," I say. "Should I put in the movie?"

"Sure," he says as he settles back onto the sofa with a sensual smile lurking across his face. I give him a coy glance and understand we probably are not going to see much of the movie tonight. The energy in the room is intoxicating as I insert the movie into the Blu-ray and join Morgan on the sofa. His handsome face draws me in like the moon draws water and before the opening credits are finished rolling across the television screen we are absorbed in a long, passionate kiss. His warm hand slides skillfully across my eager breasts and a flood of emotion dips inside of me like a roller coaster. Age-old layers of dust within me whirl into frantic life as he picks me up, carries me to my room and lays me across the bed. He enters me, and I float on a cloud of sinful elation that even the memory of a dead child or a convalescing mother cannot break.

Later we wake to the sound of wind rustling in the trees outside of my bedroom window. I check the time, its 4:45 a.m. when Morgan wakes with a smile and pulls me closer to him and kisses my forehead. I know he needs to leave soon but I lay my head on his chest and I can hear his heart beat in the most rousing, stimulating way. I lift my head to his and we once again fall into the rhythm of our erotic dance as the foliage rustles outside my window and the clouds soar above a brand new day.

10.

Pinpoints of daylight stream through my open bedroom window as I roll over onto one side and check the time once again. 6:18 a.m. I can hear Morgan in the kitchen, talking on his cell phone so I slip into a short robe and walk out of the bedroom to join him. I reach for the K-cups in the cupboard and pick up two coffee cups hanging from hooks above the sink. Morgan smiles at me as he finishes his phone call and grabs me around the waist. "Good morning," he says as he gives me a big kiss.

"Good morning," I say. "Do you have time for a cup of coffee?"

"No, I'm afraid not, I have to get going. I have to pick up a car in Albany this morning so I need to get home and take a shower and change."

"All right, I understand," I say as I return one of the two cups to its hook. "By the way, your niece's bracelet is ready."

Morgan walks into the living room and pulls the movie out of the Blu-ray and then brushes through his messy hair with his fingers. "Already? That's great. Can I stop by the shop tonight to pick it up?"

"Sure, what time do you think you'll be back in town?"

"It shouldn't take me long. I plan to be back in Syracuse by four. Will that work?"

"That's perfect, I'll watch for you," I say as I walk him to the door.

"See you then," he says, gives me another kiss and walks down the brick path to his car.

I sit on the front porch next to a large, clay pot of

purple and pink impatiens (another gift from Barbara Evans) and drink my coffee in the light of day and think about my decision to hire a hit man. I could see a counselor, like Mom has suggested several times, but, no. The idea of sitting in a stranger's office crying my heart out would never work for me and, besides, I do not want to take any medications for my depression which would most likely be recommended.

The neighborhood is starting to come to life as children exit their driveways on bicycles and roller skates. Fathers haul heavy trash cans down to the curb and the paperboy walks into the yard and hands me today's paper. I open it to the real estate section and see the listing for my house. So far we have had three showings and one couple, from New Hampshire, are close to putting in an offer according to Barbara. I peruse the weather report and see another sunny day is on tap for CNY, but a storm threatens our weekend. As I close and refold the paper I am startled when I recognize the face of the woman on page one. It is Valerie Dunne, the waitress from two nights ago. Apparently she has gone missing. According to the paper, she was last seen leaving the Onondaga Yacht Club on Sunday night. A person of interest has been taken into custody for questioning but people are asked to contact police immediately if they have any additional information regarding her whereabouts.

I close the paper and wonder if I should contact Morgan. I've never known anyone who's "gone missing" and I suspect Morgan hasn't either. After several minutes of rolling the idea around in my head. I decide to wait and talk to him about it later tonight when he comes in to pick up his niece's bracelet.

Later, when I arrive at the boutique, Orlando is wrapping up an early morning sale of a pair of turquoise earrings. I check my emails and discover that I have already received three responses to my ad for an intern. I print out the resumes of each candidate and wait for Orlando to join me behind the counter.

"We have three candidates already," I say as I retrieve the resumes off the printer. "Do you have time to look these over with me now?"

"Sure," he says, and grabs one of the resumes to read. "This one looks promising. Her name is Ellie Wilson and she lives here in Syracuse. She has just graduated from Alfred with a 4.0 and a BFA in Arts & Design. She states that working with fine metals is one of her favorite mediums."

I study the credentials of the other two candidates and frown when I realize they both live in western New York State close to the University. I'm not interested in anyone who has to make a move so I suggest we bring Ellie in for an interview right away and go from there. Orlando agrees and I send her an email suggesting an interview at 4:00 p.m. on Friday, June 21.

A fresh hive of activity floods the boutique for the rest of the afternoon and Orlando and I struggle to meet one-on-one with each customer. Before long I look up at the clock and notice it is 4:10 p.m. After the last customer leaves for the day, I walk back into the workshop and pull Morgan's bracelet from a shelf and give it one more quick polish. I place it in a custom-made teak box lined with dark purple velvet and walk back out into the showroom where I find Orlando showing Morgan the mint plant that I set in front of the window next to my desk. Swollen with the splendor of things, an all-encompassing smile graces my face, and I blush at the thought of our evening of love making the night before. "Hi," Morgan says as he leans over and gives me a kiss on the cheek. Orlando sighs behind Morgan's back and pretends to melt into the floor. *Such a clown.*

I open the box and display the bracelet which Morgan picks up and begins to inspect. "Adele, this is amazing. I thought it would be nice but, this, well, it's killer."

"I told you," Orlando adds. "Morgan, I've suggested to Deli that she make more to sell in our store. You don't have an issue with this, do you?"

"No, of course not. Waverly will have the honor of being the first one in town to own and wear an Adele Hamilton original dragonfly design," Morgan says as he returns the bracelet to its box. "How much do I owe you?"

I hesitate to talk about the money at first. It is awkward now considering how much our relationship has changed. But, finally, I say, "That will be $75, please."

"Oh, Adele," Morgan begins. "I think you are seriously undercutting yourself. This bracelet is worth at least $200."

"I agree," Orlando says quickly.

I know that the cost of the silver to make the bracelet was approximately $30 and I have a difficult time considering the inflated amount that they both suggest. "Well, how about this. For you, Morgan, it is $75, since it was you who inspired the piece. But, Orlando, for the future pieces we will charge an amount you feel is appropriate."

"That sounds good," Orlando says. Morgan smiles and pulls out a one hundred dollar bill from his wallet and hands it over to me.

I take the money, make change and thank him for his patronage. "Morgan, do you have a moment?" I ask.

"Yes, of course," he says as we step outside together. "What's up? Did you miss me?"

I smile at his boyish charm and admit I have missed him terribly but then my face takes on a serious side and I ask, "Did you see the paper this morning?"

"Yes, I did," he says. "I was shocked. Who would want to hurt Valerie?"

"I know, that's what I was thinking too," I say as we take a seat on the metal bench on the sidewalk.

"I stopped by the Club and talked to Daniel before stopping here. Apparently they picked up a homeless man who Valerie would sometimes feed leftover meals to. He was seen in the area that night, lurking about, after she left the Club."

"That's awful," I say as I cover my mouth with my hand. "I hope she is okay, the poor girl."

"Me too," Morgan says as he puts his arm around my shoulder. "It's terrible. But, hey, what are you doing for dinner tonight?"

I think about the leftover chicken salad and wine waiting for me at home and say, "nothing much, why?"

"How about I come over to your place tonight and prepare a meal for you?"

"Are you serious?" I say.

"Yes, I never joke about food," he says. "And I'm a very good cook. Do you like lobster?"

"Ah, duh," I say with a laugh. "Doesn't everyone?"

"Okay, I'll be over tonight around six and we'll eat by seven."

"No. I'm afraid that won't work. I visit my mother tonight from six to seven."

"More reason for me to make you dinner when you return," he says as his eyes dance across my face. "How about I arrive a little later, say after seven?"

"Do you need me to pick up anything?" I ask.

"Nope. Don't worry, I'll bring everything we need," he says as he kisses me gently on the lips and stands to leave.

"All right, then, see you around seven thirty," I say as I walk back into the boutique and rejoin Orlando.

"He's a keeper," Orlando says as he turns off the lights and music system for the night and we leave the boutique together, arm in arm.

11.

When I arrive at the hospital I learn that Mom has been transferred out of Intensive Care and moved into a semi-private room of her own located on the ninth floor. Her bed is at the far side of the room closest to the window overlooking the city. Mom is alone and resting peacefully when I arrive. An IV drips fluids into her veins while another machine monitors her heart rate and blood pressure. Quietly, I set down a crystal vase of pink and yellow tulips on the window sill and take a seat next to her side.

In her slumber, Mom manages to make broken look beautiful. Her dark brown hair is peppered with just the right amount of silver which frames her lovely face and falls just short of the collar line on her blue and gray checkered hospital gown. Gingerly, I lift her slender hand and rest it in between mine. Her pulse is weak and her hand is cold. I look around the room in search of another blanket when suddenly she opens her eyes and speaks to me. "Is that you, Adele? Where am I?" Her voice is strangely hoarse so I help her to a sip of water.

"Yes, it's me, Mom, and you are in your own room now," I say as she takes a small sip on her straw. "Look," I say as I gesture towards the window sill. "You've received dozens of lovely cards and flowers from your friends including some beautiful white roses from Cliff Welsh."

Mom shifts her eyes in the direction of the window and begins to smile. The right side of her face refuses to budge and her smile looks awkward and strange but I return her smile and pretend not to notice. "Are the tulips from you, Adele?"

"Yes, of course."

"You remembered. They are my favorite. Pinks and yellows, just lovely."

"How could I forget?" I say as I smile and once again lift her tiny hand into mine. Mom has always loved tulips, especially the pinks and yellows. When I was a child, I remember Mom would always buy a fresh bouquet of them for herself, every payday. When she could find them, that is.

"Do you know how long I'm supposed to be here?" she asks.

"Not yet. The doctor will be in to see you again tomorrow morning. I'm sure she will tell you then."

Mom blows a puff of air out her nose and frowns as she tries to sit up. "Let me help you," I say as I prop up a couple of pillows behind her back.

"Will you read my greeting cards to me please?" Mom asks.

"Yes, of course," I say as I pick up the first one and begin to read aloud. "This one is from Aunt Sue, who sends her very best and wants to let you know not to worry about your house. She has everything under control."

"I bet she does," Mom says as she tries to chuckle. I continue to read from the other cards until Mom once again grows weary and closes her eyes and drifts away. I sit by her side and watch her chest rise and fall for another full hour until a very large fat woman with a wide, pulpy face and a stern expression arrives in the room and informs me that visiting hours are over. I gently kiss Mom on the forehead and whisper, "I love you" before leaving her room for the night. Mom is a strong lady and I know she will survive, but I cannot help thinking about how she will feel after I'm gone. *Am I being selfish?*

* * *

A strong wind blows across the lawn as I pass through the garage door and into the house carrying a new jasmine-scented candle and a bottle of white wine. I drop my bag and packages on the kitchen counter and head back to my bedroom to change before Morgan arrives. Quickly, I slip into a cobalt-blue silk dress that matches my eyes and a pair of soft leather sandals. I apply a little pink blush to my cheeks, a fresh coat of lipstick and spray on some fresh perfume. Once finished, I stand in front of the full length mirror and turn around a few times to examine myself. I could stand to put on a couple more pounds but nothing to get excited about and my eyes look a little tired but, all and all, I look pretty good. I turn off the light in the bedroom and return to the kitchen.

Wellington soon begins his love affair with my ankles until I reach into the pantry and fill his food dish. Once he is happy eating, I light the new candle and soon the house is filled with the sweet, exotic smell of jasmine. I put the new bottle of wine into the fridge and sit down at the computer and turn on Pandora when it suddenly dawns on me that I don't know what type of music Morgan likes. There is so much I don't know about him and so little time to learn. But I settle on Van Morrison and decide if Morgan doesn't like him than we may have a problem. Just as the tender sounds of *Tupelo Honey* is released from the speakers Morgan knocks on the front door.

I open the door and discover that Morgan has come prepared. He gives me a kiss on the cheek and carries in two bags of groceries and a small cooler holding two fresh lobsters.

"Where did you get the lobsters?" I ask.

"Wegmans," he says as he tilts his head in the direction of the music. "You like Morrison too?"

"Yes, sir, Van's the man," I say and offer him a glass of half-chilled wine.

"I just took this one out of my fridge," he says as he pulls out a bottle of chilled Sauvignon Blanc from one of the grocery bags.

"Perfect," I say and take the bottle from his hands and pour us each a glass.

Morgan quickly puts me to work snapping asparagus stalks while he slices sushi-grade tuna into long narrow strips and searches for a small bowl for soy sauce and wasabi. I pull down the right size bowl and he whisks together the two ingredients, dips a thin slice of tuna into the mixture and drops it into my mouth with his fingertips. It's savory, fresh and deliciously spicy and I give him two thumbs up as I wipe my face and continue snapping the crisp asparagus into a steam pot. After we finish the fresh tuna appetizer and another glass of wine, we sit down to a meal of steamed lobster and asparagus with an arugula salad garnished with plum tomatoes, pine nuts and fresh lime dressing mixed with a little feta cheese.

"So, Adele, I was thinking. Would you like to join me this weekend for some wine tasting along the Seneca Lake Wine Trail?" Morgan asks as he dips a section of his lobster into a dish of drawn butter.

I think about how wonderful a getaway weekend in the Finger Lakes sounds but I am tormented about my plans for Labor Day. I know my death is going to hurt so many people and the more I get involved with Morgan the worse it is for him. However, even though my mind says no, my heart says yes. "That sounds interesting, when would you want to leave?" I smile as brightly as I can across the table and savor the moment.

"We'll leave on Saturday morning at nine," Morgan says and then drinks the last drop of wine in his glass and stands to open another bottle.

"I'll be ready," I say as I put down my fork and hand Morgan my empty glass. Just as he pours the wine, *Into the Mystic* seeps into the dining room, and Morgan lifts me from my chair and takes me into his arms. We dance slowly as he sings softly into my ear, every word he knows, and suddenly I am no longer certain I want to die. At least not tonight.

12.

It's Wednesday night. The night I visit Spencer's grave.

It's been a dull afternoon and gray rain clouds blanket the city like the day I met with Carl. I head south towards Belle Isle Cemetery as the wind picks up. Raindrops pattern my windshield but I have a fresh batch of buttercups, Spencer's favorite, lying on the seat beside me that I want to place on his grave.

I pull into the cemetery and step out of the car and into the rain. The tiny lake at the entrance of the cemetery looks like a tarnished mirror as raindrops the size of grapes thunder off its surface. The rain-drenched buttercups bend against the wind as I make my way to Spencer's grave.

In waves, in clouds, in big round whirls I mourn as I slump over Spencer's grave and place the buttercups next to his headstone. I say a silent prayer and tell him about Morgan and how much I think he would like him as tears roll down my checks and I suddenly feel a pang of guilt. For the first time in the eight long months since Spencer died I'm starting to imagine what life feels like again, and I know it's all because of Morgan. But I also know I can't bear not seeing my Spencer every morning, day and night. Whatever I decide, I know I am more troubled now than I was even a month ago when I first came up with the idea to hire Carl.

Carl. I think about his note and think about calling off the whole thing, but I am so torn up inside I don't know which way to turn. I flop down on Spencer's grave but tears will no longer come. I am beyond tears.

Before long, the rain stops and I watch as the sun slowly peeks out from behind a cloud. The fields of the cemetery begin to glisten like a cloth of silver, and a delightful spiciness fills the air. I look to the sky and see a young rainbow beginning to form, ripe and thick of promise. "Do you see that, Spencer? That's for you, honey," I say as I tidy up around his grave, brush the dirt from my hands and rest for a while longer.

After several peaceful minutes pass, in an incomprehensible whim of fate, a lady bug crawls on top of my leg and I know in an instant that it is Spencer. I cup the gentle creature in my hands for a long while and whisper to him, "I love you," and watch as he flies away.

I rise from the grave and head back towards my car.

I pause at the lake and think about how the waters seem to reflect a forgotten world. Many of the people buried here, I'm certain, never receive visitors but I made a promise to myself, and Spencer, that I will visit him at least once a week until the day I die.

A promise I intend to keep.

As I turn the car around and drive home, the indigo sky is swept clear of fleecy clouds and the rainbow, now a magnificent sight, stretches across the horizon in a great double arc. I pull into my driveway and know what I need to do. Tucked safely in a side pocket of my bag is the cocktail napkin with Carl's telephone number. I need to call him and tell him to call off our deal. My mother needs me and I want to live again. I want to continue getting to know Morgan and Spencer would want it this way, I just know it.

I take a deep breath and place the call.

After only one ring, I hear the following message: *The number you have dialed is no longer in service. Please check the number and dial again.* I dial the number again, 315-555-7568, and receive the same message. In a subdued panic, I get out of the car and walk through the garage and into the house. I notice I have a message waiting on my phone so I check it as I walk into the kitchen. It's from Barbara, I have an offer on the house and she needs me to call her right away. I dial Barbara's number and wait for her to pick up. "Hi, Barbara, it's Adele."

"Well, hello, I've been waiting for your call. I have some very good news. The couple from New Hampshire really wants the house. They put in a full-price offer!" She squeals.

"That's great," I say.

"Is everything all right, honey? I thought you would be a little more excited."

"Yes, I'm sorry, Barbara. I am very happy," I say. "I just returned from Spencer's grave and it takes a lot out of me, but that's very good news, what's next?"

"Assuming you accept their offer…"

"I do."

"Then it goes to the attorneys and we wait for a closing date. Congratulations, Adele. You've sold your house in less than two weeks!"

"Thank you, Barbara, it was all of your hard work," I say.

"You're welcome," Barbara says. "You'll hear from your attorney probably within a week. Let me know if I can do anything else in the meantime."

"Okay, good-bye," I say and I close my phone.

I look around the house and it feels like my old life has suddenly drifted away as I wonder about Carl's incorrect telephone number. I decide I need to drive back to Utica, to the Lounge, and see if I can find him. It shouldn't be too hard, so I feed Wellington, grab my bag, head back outside and jump into my car.

It's about an hour's drive from Syracuse to Utica so I

figure I'll be there just before dark. As I pull onto the high ramp of the thruway, the city is alive below with cars that look like multicolored ants. I quickly increase my speed and keep it steady at 75. I think about what I will say to Carl when I find him and decide that the money is not important. He can keep all of it. Hopefully he hasn't turned any of it over to the hit man (or woman) yet so that should make him happy. I just want my life back. My mother needs me, Orlando needs me and I want to continue my relationship with Morgan.

I smile as I think about selling the house. This really is good news. Now I can get an apartment, or maybe even buy a little condo in the city. I just need to find Carl and call it all off. I don't think he'll be too surprised.

I begin to relax as I think about the interview with Ellie Wilson on Friday. It's still a good idea to have a second jewelry maker so this is good news, too. For the first time since Spencer died, I'm feeling pretty good. I push in a CD into the stereo. The Black Eyed Peas, *Let's Get it Started,* begins to play and I am filled with anticipation for my new life. I will always mourn Spencer's death but I am beginning to learn how to live again with the memory of him. When I close my eyes, he is with me, as he will always be.

About thirty minutes into my drive, just east of the Turning Stone Casino, traffic reduces to a crawl and the thruway becomes a west-bound parking lot. I bang my hands on the steering wheel. "No! This can't be happening, not tonight." But there is nothing I or anyone else can do. We're jammed up. Traffic moves along at a snail's pace and it takes forty-five minutes to reach the exit for Turning Stone, a distance that should have only taken ten minutes to reach. After I pass the accident scene, a three-car pileup, I step on it and increase my speed to 80 as the sun begins to set in the distance.

Once I reach Utica it is dark and I think about turning around and going back home but I'm here now so I park my car in the same lot as before and cross the street and enter the Lounge.

Inside, the darkness stretches the entire length of the bar and it takes a few minutes for my eyes to adjust. Several men are huddled around the pool table in the back of the room; their beer bottles lined up on the shelf next to the rack of cue sticks. The jukebox is loud and I think it is playing either Lynyrd Skynyrd or AC/DC, but I can't be certain. The odor of decay flows from the sticky carpet as a skinny cocktail waitress passes by me while balancing two pitchers of frosty beer and three mugs on top of a tiny tray above her head. The bar is thick with patrons, and I recognize Dixon, the bartender, as he rushes to refill people's drinks and wipe up the many spills. I walk down to the far end of the bar and give him a wave. "What will it be sweetheart?" he asks.

"Nothing tonight, Dixon. I'm looking for Carl. Have you seen him?"

Dixon looks me up and down as he bends over the sink behind the bar and continues washing out a couple of glasses. "Do I know you?"

"Not really, but I was here last Thursday afternoon and sat in that booth right over there and met with Carl," I say as I point to the booth in the back of the bar.

"Oh, hey, I remember you. Gin and tonic, two limes, right?"

"Yes, that's right," I say. "But you didn't have any limes when I was in before. You gave me lemons."

"Well, you're in luck tonight, beautiful; I've got plenty of limes."

Encouraged that Dixon remembers me I ask again if he's seen Carl.

"No, not tonight," he says. "But it's still early; he might show up later on."

I look at the clock above the bar. It's 8:45. "What time do you think he'll be here?"

"Any time now, really," he says. "Are you sure you don't want that drink?"

I decide a drink is probably a good idea. "Okay, sure, the usual," I say with a smile and wait for Dixon to deliver my gin and tonic with two, neat lime wedges stuck to the side of the glass.

As I wait, two men and one woman offer to buy me another drink, which I politely refuse. I continue to study the clock and the door as I nurse my drink. It is 9:32 yet still no sign of Carl. Someone selects a slow song on the jukebox and couples begin to dance. I think about Morgan and suddenly wish he were here, not to dance, per se, but to help me. But how I would explain this mess to him is a mystery to me. Truth is I can't. I can never let anyone know what I've done. I just need to be sure to call it off with Carl tonight and everything will be fine. I look up from my empty glass just as the front door opens and Carl enters the bar.

I leave my seat and struggle to make my way across the dance floor as couples brush up against me. I try to reach Carl, who recognizes me immediately. I smile and he raises his hand and waives for me to join him. Someone spills a beer on my back, but I could care less as I push my way through the crowd. Finally, after much maneuvering, I reach the opposite end of the bar, closest to the door, and step two feet in front of Carl when a shot rings out and a white flash pops behind his head. Bright red blood and gray matter squirts from his forehead, right between his eyes, and splatters wildly across my face. I scream and everyone in the bar drops to the floor. Carl slumps to the ground and someone screams, "He's been shot!" Next, everyone in the bar quickly takes to their feet again and runs towards the door leaving me trampled alongside Carl's dead body.

Carl's blood carpets the floor and I'm coated in it and fragments of his former self as I struggle to find my feet. After two failed attempts, I finally stand on my own and stumble towards the door. It's all strangely surreal, as if I am watching myself try to walk for the first time in my life. I eventually make it to the door; stagger outside and into the dark. It's complete mayhem in the streets as people flee from the scene. In the distance I can hear the roar of police sirens as a rogue fire in the alleyway next to the bar snaps and pops, flinging yellow, red and white sparks high into the night sky. I manage to make my way to my car, mouth agape. My body trembles in spasms as I drive away and repeat a mantra inside my head: *Carl is dead. Carl is dead. Carl is dead.*

13.

Despite my fear, I pull together all of my scattered impulses into one adrenalin filled act and continue to drive in the direction of my home. But before getting onto the thruway and taking a ticket from the attendant, I decide I need to change my clothes. I pull into a deserted grocery store parking lot and retrieve my gym bag from the trunk of my car. With the wipes from my glove box, I erase all traces of Carl's blood from my face, neck and arms, climb into the back seat and strip away my clothing, a pair of khakis and a Bit of Silver tee-shirt. Even my shoes are caked thick with blood so I kick them off and put on a pair of clean track shoes. Once I am changed into my exercise gear, I tuck my blood-splattered hair into a baseball cap and remove my dangling earrings. I then put my bloody shoes and clothing and the spent wipes into a plastic shopping bag I find in the back seat and stuff everything into my gym bag.

It's 10:13. I need to get home.

As I drive I think about Carl and wonder why he was shot but quickly decide that in his line of business it probably comes with the territory. I shudder as I remember his black, lifeless eyes – still open when he hit the floor – and the blank expression on his face. I'm no medical examiner but I am certain he is dead. (A bullet through the brain is usually pretty definite.)

I continue to drive and my heart begins to pound inside of my throat. As far as I know, there is a hit man lurking out there somewhere with my name and address planning to gun me down over Labor Day weekend. A tidal wave of despair splashes over me as I continue to drive and try to think. I decide the only option I have is to contact Steven, in Syracuse, who set up my initial meeting with Carl. Maybe he can help me. He's my only hope.

When I pull up to my house, the stars are emerging from the blackness of the midnight sky like trusted old friends. I pull into the garage, step out of the car, remove the gym bag and shove it into the bottom of a large trash can along with the bloody floor mats. Tomorrow night, when I get home from work, I'll burn everything in the barbeque pit, but right now I need to take a shower.

I stand in the shower for twenty full minutes and let the scalding hot water burn away the images of Carl's head exploding in front of me while I rinse the blood from my hair and body. Later, I climb into bed with my cell phone and check my messages. I have two. One from Morgan and one from my real estate attorney, Cliff Welsh, who needs me to stop by his office tomorrow to drop off the abstract on my house. Morgan would like to know if I like Mexican food because he knows of good place in the city where we can eat on Friday night, if I'm available. I think about how shocked they would both be if they knew what happened to me tonight and how trivial both of their requests seem to me now.

Wellington jumps up into my bed and rests his head next to mine and begins to purr. I gently stroke his back and tell him about night's events in hushed tones and broken sobs until I fall asleep.

* * *

The next morning I wake to the sound of trash trucks clamoring outside. I jump up and throw on a robe and run into the garage. I quickly decide the trash people can take the bag with the bloody clothing and the car mats saving me the drama of having to burn them later. I open the garage door and drag the heavy can to the curb. Luckily I am not too late. The truck stops in front of my house and a young trash hauler gives me a toothy grin as he checks me out in my short, pink robe and bare feet and mindlessly tosses the bloody contents of my trash can into the back of his ugly blue truck. I thank him with a generous smile and run back up the driveway and into the garage. In the light of day, I inspect the inside of the car for any more traces of Carl's blood and quickly discover I need to wash down the steering wheel and around the dashboard. I close the garage door and get to work. Twenty minutes later I am satisfied I have erased all evidence of last night and go back into the house to take another shower and get ready for work.

It's a little later than I'd like it to be when I pull out of the driveway and finally head to work. As I make the turn onto Rt. 57 my cell phone rings. It's Orlando. "Deli, where are you?" He asks in a panic.

"I'm sorry, Orlando, I'm just leaving my house now," I say but from the sound of his voice I can tell he is upset. "Is everything all right?"

"Deli, there are two police detectives here from Utica." His voice quivers. "They want to speak to you."

I pull the car over into the McDonald's parking lot while I try to collect my thoughts. Frustration and fear dance around inside my head while I search for something to say. *Why are the police at the boutique? Why do they want to talk to me?*

"Deli?"

"Yes, Orlando, I'm still here," I say. "Did they say what they want?"

"No, they didn't. All they said is that they needed to

talk to you. Deli, what's going on? Are you in some sort of trouble?"

A heart-breaking feeling rushes over me and I want to tell him everything. I'm in deep trouble and I know it but I can't tell a soul. Not even Orlando. "No, don't worry." I say. "Please just offer them a cup of coffee and let them know I'm on my way."

"Okay. And I'll hold onto a good thought for you too, Deli girl."

"Thanks, Orlando. I'll see you in about fifteen minutes."

I think about calling my legal attorney, but she is also on the long list of people I cannot talk to about this problem. Besides, right now I have fifteen minutes to come up with a reason to justify my being at the Lounge last night. Surely, that is why the police are here. They probably want to question me about the shooting. I can handle this, I tell myself. They don't know anything about the $10,000 and the hit man. They are just investigating Carl's murder which, honestly, I know nothing about. *Calm down. Breathe. You can handle this.*

When I walk into the boutique, a very nervous Orlando and two plain-clothed detectives are waiting for me. I demonstrate an air of confidence as I smile and introduce myself and then lead the officers back into my workshop where we can be alone to talk.

The first detective, Vlad Ritter, is a squat and friendly looking man, probably about age thirty-five. He has red hair, powder blue eyes and a scruffy beard. He sits down on one of the available stools balancing a cup of coffee on his lap. His partner, Nick D'Angelo, appears to be the keener of the two, and refuses to take a seat. Detective D'Angelo is taller than Detective Ritter, probably six foot, two with black hair and dark brown eyes. Detective D'Angelo hands me his business card and then begins the questioning. "Ms. Hamilton, Detective Ritter and I are here today investigating the murder of one Carl Dennis Nardone and we have a few questions for you."

"Do you mind if I sit?" I ask.

"No, go right ahead," Detective D'Angelo says and I take a seat next to Detective Ritter.

"Ms. Hamilton, we spoke to the bar tender who was working at the Lounge last night, a Mr. Dixon Grager. In speaking to Mr. Grager, we learned that you, or someone who looks very much like you wearing a Bit of Silver tee-shirt, were present when the shooting took place last night at approximately 9:45 p.m."

I concentrate on my heart rate and posture and maintain eye contact with D'Angelo. "Yes, I was there."

"Have you ever been there before or was this your first time visiting the establishment?" D'Angelo asks.

I know he is trying to catch me in a lie, I rehearsed this in the car on the way over so I say, "Yes, I was there once before, about two weeks ago."

"And when you were there before, about two weeks ago, did you see Mr. Nardone at that time also?"

I remember to keep my answers brief and continue to maintain eye contact with him. "Yes. We had a business meeting."

"What sort of meeting?" D'Angelo asks as Detective Ritter scratches the back of his hand.

"About my boutique," I say knowing this is going to raise their suspicion.

D'Angelo and Ritter exchange glances but D'Angelo presses on. "What about your boutique?"

"It was brought to my attention that Mr. Nardone has

connections with the Turning Stone Casino and I met with him regarding the introduction of my jewelry line at their location outside of Utica."

Ritter continues to take notes in an old, beat up spiral notebook while D'Angelo stares at me for a moment. "You expect us to believe that you were dealing with Carl Nardone regarding the sale of your jewelry?"

"That's why I met with him, initially, yes," I say, prepared for his latest line of questioning.

D'Angelo finally pulls another stool over closer to where Ritter and I sit and takes a seat. "What do you mean, initially?"

"Just what it means," I say, confidently. "I initially met with Carl, Mr. Nardone, to discuss the possibility of introducing my jewelry line at the casino but then, after I had some time to think about it more seriously, I decided I did not want to branch out so I returned to the Lounge last night to let him know this."

"Why didn't you just call him?"

"I tried," I say. "But the number he gave me didn't work, so I decided it was a nice night for a drive and that I could use a drink. I had a hard day, so I drove out to the Lounge to speak to him personally."

Ritter scribbles more notes and looks over at D'Angelo as if to indicate he got it all.

"All right," D'Angelo continues. "So you're at the bar, waiting for Mr. Nardone to arrive. Did you see any strange-looking characters?"

I laugh slightly. "Have you ever been to the Lounge Detective D'Angelo? It's filled with strange-looking characters."

D'Angelo smiles and says, "Let me rephrase that. Was there anyone there that looked out of the ordinary for the

Lounge last night?"

"No."

"One last question, Ms. Hamilton and we'll be going."

"All right," I say as I smile softly.

"Would you consider yourself an eye witness to Mr. Nardone's murder?"

"No, I would not. It was too dark to see."

"Thank you," Detective D'Angelo says as he stands up. "Call me if you can think of anything else that you think may be important. You have my card."

"Yes, I will," I say as I lead them through the showroom and out the front door.

When I return, Orlando asks me if I need a hug and I tell him I need a drink.

14.

After the detectives leave the boutique, I need to get some fresh air and Orlando agrees so I decide to take a walk down to Cliff Welsh's office to drop off the abstract on my house.

Thoughts crowd my mind as I walk, but I try to push them aside when suddenly I sense someone is behind me. I turn around and see a red-haired woman, probably thirty-six, dressed all in black from head to toe riding an Olympic style bicycle while wearing dark glasses. Odd, I think, especially in a city suddenly filled with the color of summer. Initially, she is at least ten feet behind me, but she steadily increases her speed. I lift my hand to waive at her, but she dashes around me like a gazelle and becomes nothing more than an ominous blur down the city street, unnerving me. By the time I reach Cliff's office my hands are shaking.

His office is a two-story circa 1800s house located on the fringe of Armory Square. Victorian in style, the house has a steeply pitched roof of irregular shape with siding painted in period colors of beige, cream and bronze. It features a striking and intricate turret which looms large above the front door and includes a full-width asymmetrical porch that wraps around the house from center to left. Once inside, I climb the grand mahogany steps to the second floor and arrive at Cliff's office where I knock once before entering.

The office is as impressive as the house itself – complete with deep, rich mahogany book cases that frame the ample room and stretch from floor to ceiling. Hundreds of leather bound books line the many shelves: countless law manuals, encyclopedias, dictionaries, thesauruses and a few century-old novels. An equally expensive-looking desk, with majestic claw feet and a black leather blotter, is positioned squarely in the center of the room. Beneath it rests a very large navy blue, gold and cream colored Persian rug which anchors the room. Cliff's chair, made up of soft, supple brown leather appears to be slightly worn, marking its age. The room is tastefully decorated and smells of century old wood and musk that tickles my senses.

Cliff is an old friend of the family and his presence puts me at ease the minute I walk into his office. He possesses a charming air of vigor and vitality for a man of sixty-two and every time I meet with him I secretly wish he would call my mother and ask her out on a date. He is dressed in a brown suit and a salmon colored dress shirt which matches his tie, a bit too wide for this decade, but he smiles and stands the moment I enter the room. He speaks in an accent warm with milk and honey as he gives me a two-handed hand shake. "Good morning, Adele, how are you this glorious Thursday morning?"

"Living the dream," I say, ironically speaking for my own twisted pleasure.

"Well, congratulations on the quick sale of your home. Houses are sitting on the market for months and sometimes years these days. You are a very lucky girl."

"Yes, I'm a lucky girl all right," I say as Cliff looks around his desk and confesses to being a bit disorganized. He finally finds the file on the sale of my house and drops the abstract inside. "Is there anything else you need from me at this point, Cliff?"

"No, not at this time. The closing is currently scheduled for Friday, August 15th at 9:00 a.m."

"Here?" I ask.

"Yes, right here, my lady," Cliff says as he lifts up my hand and gently kisses the back of it. Cliff has always been a charmer and incredibly kind to me. "Adele, please do not think I am asking out of mere curiosity, but I heard about your mother. How is Sarah?"

"She's doing much better. As a matter of fact, I pick her up from the hospital later today." Words which instantly bring a smile to my face.

"Please send her my regards, would you please?" He says with great blue eyes fixed in watery adoration.

A strange flutter of expansion in my heart takes over and I say, "Cliff, why don't you give my mom a call sometime? I'm sure she would love to see you."

Cliff makes his way back to his desk and takes a seat in his leather chair and looks out the window. "Maybe I will, Adele, maybe I will."

I leave him alone with the thought of my lovely mother on his mind as I walk three doors down to the Armory Tobacco Shop, which is owned and operated by Steven Nardone. Steven is a general acquaintance of mine and the one who told me of the whereabouts of his uncle's establishment.

As I step inside the shop, I am instantly surrounded by the rich, cedar-like smell of tobacco, like stepping into a giant humidor. There are shelves holding boxes of brightly-wrapped cigars, tables covered with jars of pipe tobacco and walls lined with specialty pipes. I simply love the smell of tobacco even though I have never smoked a day in my life and didn't care for the smell of my father's cigarettes. There is no justifiable cause for my infatuation, but I soak up the deliciousness of it all while I wait for Steven to finish with a customer.

Once we are alone in the shop, I approach Steven, a

lean and neurotic looking man, and give him a look of desperation. "What's wrong?" he asks.

"I take it you heard about your uncle's death?"

"Yes, I heard. Dumb bastard. That's what he gets for living that type of lifestyle."

"Yea, I guess," I say as I look around the store some more, eyes seeking anything other than his as I try to come to my point. "Steven, I met with your uncle last week and, well, without going into detail I made some arrangements with him."

"Adele, I'm sure I don't want to know what you discussed."

"Right," I say as I select a random pipe from the wall display and set it down on the counter. I don't smoke but I'm suddenly so nervous I grab something to buy, anything, to somehow substantiate why I'm there. "Anyway, I've changed my mind and I need to talk to someone in his organization, I mean, about our previous arrangements," I pause. "Do you know any of the names of his business associates?"

By the grimaced look on Steven's face, I get the strong impression that he doesn't get too involved in the family business and therefore cannot help me, but I wait for him to answer. "No, Adele, I don't. I gave you his name and location but that's as far as I go. I'm sorry," he says as he fills some more jars with pipe tobacco. "Look around. I'm a respectable businessman."

I look around the shop and understand. He can't help me. "Just this," I say as I slide the pipe across the counter.

"I didn't know you smoked, Adele."

"I don't," I say as I pay for the pipe and then leave the shop.

* * *

After Orlando and I close the boutique for the day, I head over to Upstate to pick up Mom. On my way to the car, I decide to send Morgan a quick return text from last night.

Me: I love Mexican but, sorry, busy tomorrow night.

Morgan: Who's the guy, I'll kill him.

Me: Funny, LMAO

Morgan: Rain check?

Me: You got it. BTW, having dinner with Mom tomorrow night.

Morgan: Still on for this weekend?

Me: Yes

Morgan: See you at 9.

Me: OK

I shut my phone and walk to the dry cleaners to drop off my dress and chat with Mrs. Clark about my mother's condition for a long while before finally heading back towards my car. As I continue to walk across the square I spot the red-headed woman once again on the bicycle, eating me up behind dark glasses. I hesitate. *Could this be the hit person?* With great trepidation, I walk towards her, slowly, and ask, "May I help you?"

She shakes her head 'no' and jumps onto her bicycle and rides away.

"Who are you?" I scream but she keeps pedaling and in a few seconds she is gone.

Who is this woman? I wonder as I drive towards the hospital. Then it suddenly dawns on me that this is what my life has become; an ugly sea of paranoia. Everywhere I look now I find myself searching for something or someone that may or may not be there. But he, or she, is there, somewhere. I can feel it. But I have no idea where he or she may strike, or what I'm going to do to prevent it. My life has an expiration date stamped on top of it, carefully prearranged by me with the help of a deceased gangster, and there seems to be nothing I can do about it now.

As I continue to drive I think about leaving town. I could visit Deirdre, but she has three young children, all under the age of ten and I can't imagine putting them in any danger. *What would I tell my mother and Orlando, or even Morgan? Would I simply just vanish?* I decide to put it out of my mind for a while as I pull into the hospital parking lot and go inside to collect my mother.

15.

When Mom and I enter her house we can hear the slosh and clink of dishes being washed in the kitchen sink. Mom needs the use of a walker now to get around, but she is already a pro and quickly makes her way into the kitchen and begins to berate her sister. "Sue, why the heck are you washing those damned dishes by hand? You know I have a dishwasher."

"Well, it's nice to see you, too," Aunt Sue says as she removes her hands from the sudsy water and gives Mom a big hug. "I hate those Goddamn machines and you know it," she says as she returns to the sink. I set down my bag and keys on the kitchen counter and smile in admiration of their peculiar relationship and love.

"Are you staying for dinner tonight?" Mom asks.

"No, I can't tonight," Aunt Sue explains. "I've got my book club at 6:00 and you know I never miss it."

Mom rolls her eyes at me as if to excuse Aunt Sue and her routines. Aunt Sue grocery shops on Tuesdays, bowls on Wednesdays and attends her book club meetings on Thursday nights. It's all very much cast in stone and it drives Mom crazy.

"Can you join us tomorrow night, Aunt Sue?" I ask.

"You betcha! And I'll be doing the cooking, too."

"Great," Mom and I say in unison and just like that, Aunt Sue's plans for tomorrow night are set.

After Aunt Sue leaves, Mom gets settled in watching Family Feud on the television in her bedroom while I begin preparing us something to eat. I find a bag of frozen meatballs and a jar of tomato sauce but no spaghetti so I grab my keys and bag off of the kitchen counter and tell Mom I have to run to the grocery store.

As I drive, I listen to the local radio station and am shocked to learn that Valerie Dunne is still missing but still no solid leads. I gasp and wonder about the homeless man. Apparently he is no longer a suspect. Once again I think about my own immortality and the ticking clock counting down to Labor Day. I need to talk to someone. It can't be Mom, she is too fragile now and besides, she couldn't help me. Same with Orlando, he would become hysterical and duck every time the front door of the boutique opened thinking if it was the gunman. Aunt Sue is just too old, and I cannot talk to the law.

I walk into Wegmans grocery store and decide it should be Morgan that I tell my dark secret to. It may mean the end of a budding relationship, but in my heart I think I can make him understand my state-of-mind at the time I first met Carl. I was desperate to die, but when I met him and fell in love and...*wait, did I just say love?*

I stand in line at the checkout counter. *Am I in love with Morgan Spencer?* My mind is racing with ideas but, regardless, everything has changed, dramatically, since the first time I met with Carl Nardone and maybe Morgan can help me. After all, my life is at stake.

When I arrive back at Mom's house, I prepare our dinner without any trouble. As we sit down together at the kitchen table and begin to eat, I tell her about my meeting with Cliff, and that he sends his regards.

"That's nice," Mom says without looking up from her plate. "How did he look?"

"Handsome and as charming as ever," I say as I try to decide whether or not to tell her I asked him to give her a call. As I take another bite of my spaghetti, Mom sets down her fork and begins to cry. "Mom, what is it? Are you in pain?"

"No, it's not that, I'm fine, physically speaking."

"What is it then?"

With the use of her walker, Mom stands up from the table and slowly walks over to the kitchen sink and gazes out the window into the back yard. The light of day is melting away and the mellow sunset is just settling in. Mom takes a deep breath and turns around to face me. "Adele, there is something I've been meaning to tell you, but I just haven't been able to find the correct time."

"Go on."

Mom sits down again and interlocks her fingers and rests her hands on top of the table. "I don't know where to begin," she says. She looks like a five-year-old child and I want to hold her.

"Mom, it's okay. You can tell me anything," I say, trying to reassure her.

"Adele, when your father and I were first married, I had an affair..."

"Mom, you don't need to tell me this," I say, suddenly mortified.

"Yes, I do," Mom says as she continues. "Oh heck, I'm just going to come right out with it and then you can ask me any questions you may have."

"All right," I say, absolutely certain I no longer want to know what she has to say.

"Adele, Cliff was the man I had the affair with."

I sit perfectly still, like a stone wall until my eyes suddenly grow larger and begin to operate on cruise control; rotating slowly from left to right. "Wwwhat?" I manage to say.

Mom dips her head and shrugs her shoulders. "Yes, it's

true and there is more. Adele, Cliff and I have been seeing each other for a few months now."

I try to wrap my head around this news while I remove the talons from my heart. I stand up from the table and begin to wonder if there is a black cloud following me around. "Mom, I don't know what to say."

"Do you disapprove?"

"Of the affair, yes. Of the relationship now, no."

"Are you sure?"

"Yes, of course. I've always thought you and Cliff would make a good couple. Like I said, I'm not happy to learn of the affair, but, nothing can be done about that now, right? So let's forget about it."

"Right," Mom says as I help her back to her seat and we finish our meal.

16.

When I was a young child, I used to lie awake listening to my parents argue outside my bedroom window as they sat side by side on the front porch stoop. My father would play his guitar, smoke his cigarettes and drink a lot of beer while Mom, a teetotaler, constantly complained about his drinking and partying.

We lived in a modest townhouse development called Empire Court where the houses – four styles in all – were lined up in long rows, each painted a different color. Ours, one of the smaller units, was a cool gray with burgundy shutters and a very shiny black front door. I don't think Mom and Dad ever caught on to my eaves dropping late at night, but I remember secretly wishing they would so the arguing would stop. But it never did.

One night, in the summer of 1990, I remember a particular argument that grew increasingly bitter as the sun set low outside my bedroom window.

"Where were you last night?" Dad asked as he plucked his guitar and played an old Hank Williams tune from memory.

"What do you mean, where was I? I was working, like always," Mom said. "You do remember working, right Dick?"

"Screw you, Sarah," Dad fired back. "You know I'm trying to find a new job but it takes time. You got home pretty late last night, later than usual."

"I went out with some of my friends, is all. I suppose you have a problem with that now, too?" she said.

"What friends? And don't try to tell me it was with the

ladies from your bible group because I'm not buying it. It was well past midnight when I heard you sneak up the steps," Dad said as he continued to strum his guitar.

Mom remained silent for a while so I got up and peeked out the window, being careful not to let them see me.

"So? Are you going to tell me who you were with?" Dad asked again.

"I went to a movie with Tina, my friend from work."

"Oh yea, what movie did you see?"

Again there was a long silence as Mom stood up from the stoop and picked a cherry blossom from the tree in our front yard. Even I knew she was lying but I didn't understand why. *Why would Mom lie?* "We went to see *Ghost*," she finally said. "The one with Patrick Swayze and Demi Moore."

Dad finished the *Cheatin' Heart* song and began playing something I didn't recognize. "Okay, then, tell me what the movie is about and don't say 'a ghost'," Dad said as he began to tune his guitar.

"What do you care what the movie was about?" Mom asked as she rejoined Dad on the front stoop.

"Because I think you're lying, Sarah," Dad said as his voice grew louder.

"Well maybe I am lying but it's not like you care. You never touch me anymore."

At this point I climbed back into my bed and pulled the covers up over my head, but despite my efforts, I could still hear them talking.

"Maybe I would touch you if you weren't always bitching at me every goddam minute!" Dad shouted.

A loud silence fell over the night when I heard Mom say, "Do you want a divorce, Dick, is that what you are really asking me here?"

Dad never answered this question but it burned a hole through my juvenile soul that I never could erase. Dad gathered up his guitar and his cigarettes and beer and walked back inside the house, slamming the door as Mom remained seated on the front stoop with the cherry blossom tucked behind her ear. And then a sound I never heard before resonated way down low inside a place I did not know as Mom began to cry.

17.

The next morning the sun shines sporadically over my house and the wind chimes clang loudly through the open bedroom window. Today, Orlando and I are scheduled to interview Ellie Wilson at four o'clock, so I decide to dress a little more professionally, forgo the typical shop tee-shirt and put on an oatmeal-colored suit. As I apply my make-up I think about my deep blue eyes and how Mom's and Dad's eyes are both brown. I still cannot believe that Cliff Welsh and my mother had an affair. But, I have to admit, things are starting to add up. *Could Cliff be my biological father?* We are both left-handed, we both keep a messy desk and we have these unmistakably similar cobalt-blue eyes. I shake my head as I wonder what other traits we may share and then decide I can't think about that right now. I have bigger problems. So I forget about Cliff and leave the house.

When I step into the garage I am surprised to find Wellington sound asleep on the cement floor. "How'd you get out here, big guy?" I ask, but, as usual, Wellington ignores me. He's a heavy cat so I set my bag down on the garage floor before I bend over to pick him up. It isn't until I lift him that I realize that he is cold and stiff. But much to my shock and horror, I turn him over to discover that his eyes have been gouged out and that he is very much dead. I cradle him in my arms and begin to scream.

And then I dial 911.

Once the police arrive, they help me secure my windows and doors, and tell me they will keep an eye on the house for a few days but probably it was just some sick joke played on me by some disturbed, teenage boys that live in the apartment complex behind my house. I think about the hit man and wonder if I should tell the officers when one of them breaks my concentration. "We've had a lot of trouble with these kids lately, now that school is out for the summer and all."

"So sorry about your cat," the other officer says. "Do you want us to take him away?"

"No, I want to bury him. But thank you. You'll let me know if you catch whoever did this, right?"

"Yes, ma'am, we will," the first officer says before he and his partner leave and I am once again alone with a very dead Wellington.

I decide I need to call Orlando and tell him I can't make it in to work today and ask him to meet with Ellie alone. He agrees. I then call Morgan to see if he is available to help me bury Wellington.

"What?!" Morgan says after I explain to him what's happened. "I'll be right there…"

"Thanks, Morgan – I'm scared," I say as I cry into the phone.

"I don't blame you, fucking kids! Keep the doors and windows locked, and I'll be right there."

"I will."

After I set down the phone, I change out of my business suit and into a pair of faded jean shorts and an old Alfred U tee-shirt then sit down at the kitchen table to wait for Morgan. *Would a hit man do this, kill a cat? Is this some type of weird warning?* I'm filled with horror when, finally, fifteen minutes later Morgan is at my front door. I open the door and begin to cry. He comes inside and rocks me gently in his arms. "Who would want to hurt an innocent old cat like Wellington?" I ask.

"Someone with a very sick mind," he says as he

continues to rock me. "Do you want me to take care of him?"

I dry my eyes and break free from his embrace. "I would like you to help me bury him, if you would."

"Of course. Where do you want to bury him?"

"I don't know. Normally I would say here, out back, but now that I'm selling the house that doesn't make much sense."

"I know the perfect place," he says. "Now you have a seat while I wrap him up. Do you have an old towel or something I can use?"

I walk to the hall closet and pull down a box containing my fine linen tablecloths and select one similar to the color of Wellington's eyes. "Use this," I say as Morgan takes it from my hands and disappears into the garage for a few minutes. When he returns, carrying Wellington bundled in his arms, we walk out the front door and lock it.

"Where are we going?" I ask as Morgan puts Wellington in the trunk of his car.

"To my parent's place, outside Baldwinsville. They have a farm with twenty acres. It's beautiful and bright, with lots of animals. I think Wellington would like it there. It's where I buried all of my pets growing up. It's the only place I can think of."

I think about this and am not sure I want my cat buried at a stranger's farm but I have nowhere else to take him so I agree. "Are you sure your parents won't mind?" I ask.

"Positive," he says as we continue to drive. "They love animals."

"Great." I close my eyes and let the spray of the wind cover my face as Morgan drives.

When we arrive at the Spencer family farm, we enter the property by way of a tree-lined driveway where splotches of shadows are cast by the mighty maples that ripple through the open sun roof. The leafy arches of the tall trees extend for a good two-hundred yards until we come to a dead end at the mouth of circular driveway where an exquisite, Italianate farmhouse lays in wait. Morgan pulls around the drive and parks and we step out from the car together.

The wind fills the trees with a rustling murmur and a breeze skims my neck as I look around. In the sunniest part of the lawn, behind the house, there is a small pond with a dock and a diving board. Beyond the pond lies a small orchard; a mix of both apple and cherry trees. And further still is a red barn with no silo. Two brown and white horses graze in an open field. "This is breathtaking," I say. "Wellington will love it here."

"Good," Morgan says. "Let's go say hello to my folks."

Inside, the house smells of polished wood and lavender. Twelve-foot ceilings boast original tongue and groove paneling and the walls are covered with tastefully selected and modern flowered wallpaper. I ask Morgan if I should remove my shoes when I see the highly-polished hardwood floors. "Don't be silly," he says. "Come on, this way."

He leads me through the foyer and down a grand hallway until we reach the kitchen where we find his mother and father sitting at the table playing gin rummy.

"Glad you're here, Morgan," his mother says. "Your father is cheating again."

"I am not cheating, Sylvia, stop saying that or you're likely to scare away this beautiful young lady," his father says as he smiles and stands up. "Forrest Spencer," he says as he extends his hand to me. He is tall, like Morgan, but a little rounder around the middle. His gray hair is full and flattering and he smells of Old Spice and pipe tobacco.

"Glad to meet you. Adele Hamilton," I say as I return his smile and shake his hand.

Morgan's mother stands up from the table, slowly walks over to me and looks me up and down as if I'm here for her inspection.

"Mother," Morgan says. "Don't be rude."

"I'm not being rude, you are. Aren't you going to introduce me to this exquisite creature?"

"Sorry," Morgan begins. "Mother, I'd like you to meet Adele Hamilton." He pauses. "Adele, this is my mother, Sylvia Spencer." Sylvia has a face tightened like a mask with eyes reduced to sharp points, ready to pierce any lies. She is dressed in blue satin lounging pajamas and doused with lavender perfume, and it is difficult not to see the resemblance to Morgan. He is the spitting image of his mother, who appears to be somewhere between sixty and dead. I stand trapped in her sight line of glacial blue eyes before I summon the courage to speak.

"Very nice to meet you, Mrs. Spencer, what a lovely home you have," I say.

"Thank you," she says as she returns her gaze to Morgan. "To what do we owe the pleasure of your company, Morgan?"

I feel myself begin to perspire and wish upon all wishes that we had not come here today to bury my dead cat.

"We'd like to bury Adele's cat here, if you wouldn't mind, Mother."

Sylvia looks at me with a faint, wistful smile which lightens her brooding face. "Oh, my dear, I am so sorry. What happened to your kitty?"

"Just this morning I discovered him lying dead in the garage." I don't tell her about the gouged out eyes. "He was old, thirteen."

"Well, of course you may bury him here. All of the deceased family pets are buried here."

"Thank you," I say and it is settled. Morgan takes me by the hand and leads me out of the house.

"Sorry about that," he says when we get to his car. "Mother can be very dramatic, but she loves animals. I told you it would be okay."

"I get the distinct feeling that she loves my poor Wellington more than she likes me."

"Don't worry, she'll warm up. She always does."

After we bury Wellington and I say a silent prayer over his little grave, we walk back up to the house to say goodbye to Morgan's parents. When we re-enter the house, Forrest is in the living room reading the newspaper but Sylvia has retired upstairs to take a nap. We sit and visit with Forrest for a little while and I find him charming, much like his son, with an air of calmness and dignity. I learn that he served in the Korean War as a pilot and worked for Lockheed Martin in Syracuse for forty years. I like him instantly.

"Thank you, again, Mr. Spencer, for allowing me to bury my cat here. I'm sure he will be very happy."

"You are welcome. But, please, call me Forrest, everyone does," he says as he puts an arm around me and gives me a little squeeze.

"All right, Dad, keep your hands off," Morgan jokes and we say good-bye and walk through the parlor where, in the corner of the room, sits a grand piano.

"Do you play?" I ask Morgan as I motion towards the piano.

"Yes, I learned how to play the piano when I was young but my sister, Maria, is the expert," he says as he lifts his chin in the direction of the piano. I walk closer to the piano and notice the portrait of a woman set in a silver frame. I breath in as I lift the picture into my hand for a closer look. I begin to tremble inside as I study the photograph and think I'm going to be sick, but I regain my composure, set the frame down. I recognize her, I'm sure. It's the red-haired woman I saw riding her bike in Armory Square.

18.

The drive back to my house is very silent for several minutes as I try to decide whether or not to tell Morgan I saw his sister riding her bike in Armory Square yesterday.

Morgan finally breaks the silence. "Hey, I was thinking. Since you are off today, how about we make it a three-day weekend and leave for the Finger Lakes today instead of tomorrow?"

I stare out my window and think about the fact that I am supposed to have dinner with Mom and Aunt Sue tonight and poor Orlando all alone interviewing Ellie Wilson back at the boutique when rain begins to sprinkle the windshield. I put my window up and think about how desperately I want to get out of town for a few days and try to forget about everything. "So, what do you think?" Morgan asks again.

"That sounds like a good idea," I say. "I could use some rest and relaxation."

"Great," Morgan says. "Let's swing by your house first, so you can pack, and then we'll stop by my place. Sound like a plan?" He turns his head and smiles at me.

"Yes," I say as I turn away from him and watch the rain race down my window.

After I pack, I call my mother and Orlando and let them both know I'll be out of town for the weekend and will see them on Monday. Orlando is jealous, Mom is worried but I am suddenly excited. Three whole days of rest and relaxation. I can hardly wait. Now I am anxious to get to Morgan's place so he can pack, and we can finally be on the road.

Morgan lives in a small cottage he rents close to Onondaga Lake not too far from the city. We step out of the car and I am suddenly filled with the deepest desire to see the inside of his house. Up until now I have not been invited to his home and I cannot wait until we reach the front door. The weathered siding is painted river blue and the front door is a bright, cheerful yellow. Along the cobblestone path are several types of plants I cannot identify. Some are bright green, some are all blooms and others, well, look quite exotic. We reach the front door, but before Morgan inserts his key into the lock he turns around and asks, "Do you have any seasonal allergies?"

"What?" I ask with a puzzled look on my face.

"You know, allergies. Do you get hay fever?"

"No, why?" I ask.

"You'll see," Morgan says as he opens the front door.

The cottage is flooded with light and resting on every single surface is one type of potted plant or another. In the foyer, stands a six-foot cactus surrounded by smaller plants arranged in simple, orange clay pots. In the kitchen, hanging from silver chains, are dozens of herb plants with even more pots on the window sills: basil, chicory, rosemary and thyme, to name a few. In the living room, instead of books, are rows and rows of plants scattered about the room; orchids, roses, daisies, bromeliads and ferns. "Morgan, this is amazing," I say not knowing where to look next.

"Thanks," he says as he picks up a pink Gerber daisy and hands it to me. "This one is for you."

I take the hardy little plant into my hands and look at it with sincerest gratitude. "Thank you, Morgan, this is beautiful."

"You're welcome. You can leave it here for the weekend. We'll pick it up on the way back home."

"Okay," I say. "How long did it take you to do all this?"

"Well, some plants are new this spring but others, like the cactus in the foyer, are very old; I've had that one for fifteen years."

"Amazing," I say again as I continue to look around the room. "I never would have guessed you had a green thumb."

"Ah, but I do," he says and he pulls me closer. We begin to dance around the living room while he hums and I think we may never get on the road.

* * *

As Morgan drives, I think about Maria again and decide I should just tell him that I saw her yesterday. It would be weird if I didn't tell him, and it's probably no big deal so I come right out with it. "Hey, I saw your sister in Armory Square yesterday."

Abruptly, as if someone rose up out of the steering wheel and choked him with two hands, Morgan pulls the car over to the side of the road and turns his upper body to face me. "What?! What did she say to you?"

"She didn't say anything, that's just it."

"What do you mean? Tell me everything. What did she do?"

My brain grinds its gears as I try to figure out why he is suddenly so perturbed. But obviously my first instinct was correct; there is something strange about Maria. "She was riding her bike the first time I saw her."

"You saw her more than *once*?" He shouts.

"Yes, a few hours apart, each time in the square."

"Tell me everything," he says again. His voice is agitated.

"I'm trying to."

"Okay, I'm sorry. It's just that my sister is a royal pain in my ass and I get a little crazy when I hear about her. Go on."

"As I was saying, the first time I saw her it was about 10:00 a.m. I was walking from the boutique to my attorney's office and she was behind me. Of course, at the time I didn't know it was your sister."

"Of course not."

"So anyway, she starts gaining on me and I was a little afraid she was going to run me over with her bike so I waved to be sure she saw me. Then she blazed by me and raced away. That's it."

"Fuck."

"Morgan, what's wrong?"

Morgan rubs his hands along his thighs and looks down at his lap. "My sister is mentally ill, and it's been a battle keeping her sane. We are twins and she kind of worships me. To the point that whenever I have a girlfriend she gets a little over protective of me. That's why my relationship with Valerie Dunne didn't work out. According to Valerie, Maria kept showing up at her job and pestering her. Valerie couldn't take it any longer, so we broke up. I'm afraid she'll try to poison our relationship as well."

"Why didn't you tell me about this sooner?" I ask.

"Oh, right. Hi, my name is Morgan Spencer and my sister is a fucking fruit cake who may stalk you. Would you care to go out on a date with me?"

"I see your point."

"You said you saw her again?"

"Yes, later on, when I was leaving work for the night. She was standing near my car, leaning against her bike. I recognized her from earlier, so I called out to her and asked if I could help her with something. She shook her head 'no' and rode away. That's it. End of story."

Morgan leans back in his seat and rubs both of his eyes with the palm of his right hand. "Listen, Adele, my sister may try to break us up. She's done it before. She'll tell you terrible lies about me. Anything to get you to go away. You mustn't believe a word she says, and you must call me anytime you see her around, okay? Promise me."

"Okay, Morgan, I promise. But you're starting to scare me. Is she dangerous?"

"I'm not sure..."

I think for a minute and then blurt out, "Do you think she killed my cat?"

"I don't know," Morgan says. "Maybe."

I lean back in my seat and realize that I am totally fucked. Not only could Maria have killed my Wellington, but she could, possibly, be associated with Carl. "Morgan, I have something I need to talk to you about as well. I'm in trouble."

"What sort of trouble?"

The traffic on the thruway continues to blaze by us and I turn and look at the busy road. I do not want to talk to him about this now, not here. "Can it wait until we get to the hotel, or maybe over dinner?" I ask. "I don't want to talk about it in the car."

"Sure, of course," he says as he puts the car back into gear and pulls out onto the highway. "But we're not staying at a hotel."

When we arrive in Geneva, I remember Spencer at the age of nine playing on the northern shore of Seneca Lake with Lonnie. They are building sand castles and flying a kite while I take endless photographs. It's sunny and warm, like it is now, and I am happy. "Are you hungry?" Morgan asks, breaking me from my flashback.

"Sure, I could eat."

"Okay, let's eat here, instead of in Watkins. We'll eat there tomorrow night at a little Mexican place I know."

"Sounds good," I say. Morgan parks the car along Exchange Street, and we get out and head into town.

On our way to dinner, we find the streets are alive with dozens of street musicians and hundreds of appreciative patrons. We eagerly join a crowd gathered around an old blues player; a talented black man with wrinkled skin, like shoe leather, and crystal blue eyes and silver-white hair. His clothes are old and tattered as is the equally old Dobro that stretches across his lap. We watch as he stomps his feet and skillfully makes that old Dobro sing, rocking his head from left to right while rejoicing as strangers drop money into his open guitar case. Morgan bends over and drops a five dollar bill into the collection. The old man bows his head and smiles at us both as we walk away.

"What did the sign say?" I ask.

"Waldo's Retirement Fund," Morgan answers as we walk onto the next musician before finally stopping in at *Parker's* for dinner.

Once we are seated, I ask, "We're not staying in a hotel?"

"Nope. I rented us a private cottage in Dresden," Morgan says with a toothy grin. "I hope you'll like it."

"Where is Dresden?"

"It's about half way down the lake, on the western shore, about a fifteen minute drive from here. After we eat we'll get checked in."

"Okay, great," I say when I realize I'm starving. "The burgers look yummy."

"Get one, that's what I'm having, a burger and a beer."

After our burgers and beers arrive, Morgan leans back in the booth and asks, "So, Adele, you said you needed to talk to me?"

I begin to fumble like a child with my burger as I realize I'm still not ready to talk to him about it. If ever. It's too dark, too terrible. I can't expect him to understand. Why I ever thought I could expect him to understand is now beyond me so I change the subject. "These burgers are fantastic."

"Yea, they're pretty good," Morgan says as he stares across the booth at me. "You're not ready to tell me, are you?"

"No," I say as I look down at my lap.

"Okay, that's fine, but I'm here when you are ready, okay?"

"Thanks, Morgan. When I'm ready, I'll let you know."

After dinner we walk back to the car and find the streets deserted. All the musicians have packed up and gone home, less one. The old blues player is still sitting on the same corner playing his Dobro and stomping his feet without a soul around to hear. Calmness overcomes me as I realize that sometimes it's not about the money or the crowds but simply the joy that one can experience all alone. I smile at the wise, seasoned old musician as he smiles back at me and I know he knows that I understand.

19.

When I was twelve, I held my first piano recital at my middle school, Onondaga Hill, located just west of Syracuse. I practiced my piece, *Night Horsemen*, for weeks and weeks and I was looking forward to seeing my parents watch me from the audience. Especially Dad, as he was the musician in the family. I wanted him to feel proud as he watched me take the stage.

I wore a fancy black skirt with white polka dots that Mom had purchased for me just days before from Macy's. With it I wore a simple, black leotard top and black lace stockings that looked absolutely marvelous against the white backdrop of the stage. My long blond hair was tied neatly in a single braid that fell over my right shoulder. As I took the stage, the sound of my shiny new shoes clicking across the hard wooden floor is all you could hear as a hush fell over the crowd. Bravely, I stood and faced them and announced my name and the name of my piece. I was ready.

But before taking my seat at the piano, I scanned the crowd for Mom and Dad. Finally, in the fourth row, behind a very plump woman in a purple dress, sat my Mom and Cliff Welsh. But no Dad. Mr. Welsh pointed up to me and gave me a silent 'thumbs up' as I bowed my head in acknowledgment of his gesture and reluctantly took my seat at the baby grand.

I tried to play but for the first time in my life, I felt nervous. Really nervous. My heart began to beat rapidly and my palms began to sweat. I was in unfamiliar territory.

I drew a deep breath and sat quietly on the bench as I tried to remember the song but it was impossible. I forgot the opening bars and couldn't strike a key.

The crowd grew increasingly quiet as the seconds ticked by, waiting patiently for me to begin playing. I could see my piano instructor, trying to mouth the first notes behind the heavy curtain but my mind went blank and I began to cry.

Again I scanned the crowd for my dad, but he was not there. Just Mom and Mr. Welsh who sat stoned faced with their mouths agape looking straight at me. I ran from the stage, distraught, knowing full well that Dad had forgotten about the recital.

And me.

20.

Morgan was right. Dresden was about a fifteen minute drive from Geneva on a state route lined with acres and acres of grapevines that stretched along the sloping hills surrounding the lake. Dresden has one stop light, a Dairy Queen, an old pub called the Dresden Hotel and endless rows of cottages lining the shore of Seneca Lake. Morgan makes his way to Arrowhead Beach Road and we pull up to cottage No. 406. As we step out of the car the sun sets and transforms into fragrant twilight. The moon shines over the lake and the water glistens.

Inside the cottage, there are two bedrooms and one great room with a pull-out sofa. We decide to sleep in the great room, on the sofa, across from the row of large windows overlooking the lake.

I'm surprised to discover that I am tired, really tired, and I fall asleep easily while Morgan plays his guitar into the wee hours of the night. I do not know how long I am asleep before I begin to dream, but I have a terrible nightmare. I dream that Spencer has come for me, not as my son, but as the hit man. He points a gun in my face and tells me I'm about to die. I try to tell him that I love him and to put the gun down but he waves it in the air and fires off two warning shots. I wake up screaming, and Morgan picks me up and holds me in his arms, "hush, hush, you were only dreaming." And I know I need to tell him about the hit man but when I try, I cannot. Instead I tell him about my fear of finding Wellington dead and the stress of my mother's stroke and, of course, always the pain I carry around in my heart every day over the death of Spencer. Morgan seems to understand and strokes my hair, and we make love for the next few hours until the sun slowly begins to rise over the eastern shore of the lake. Once the sun shines brightly into our room, we roll over and fall asleep in each other's arms and I think I'm never going to tell him about Carl Nardone.

Later that morning an unseasonable, piercing cold wind blows off of the lake and into the living room, waking me. I stand and walk to the window and watch as scores of small waves crash to the shore while Morgan lies sleeping. His vulnerable nude body is completely exposed to the cold so I cover him with a blanket. Quietly, I make a cup of coffee, wrap another blanket around me and step outside. I sit down on the edge of the dock and let the warm sun freckle my face. The cool water ripples over my bare feet while I sip the hot coffee and wonder what I'm going to do next.

I take another sip and think about Cliff Welsh, my mother's lover, whom, up to two days ago I knew nothing about. *Should I tell him? No.* I answer immediately and laugh out loud at the ridiculousness of the suggestion when I hear Morgan sneaking up behind me on the dock. "What's so funny?" he asks as he takes a seat next to me.

"Oh, nothing, just laughing at myself," I say as I look out across the lake.

"Chilly morning," Morgan says as he wraps the blanket around himself a bit tighter and takes a long sip of my coffee.

I watch as a quick shiver ruffles the brooding stillness of the water, then I begin. "Morgan..."

"Yes?"

"I'm ready to talk to you. I'm in trouble and I need to tell someone, but it's not the kind of thing that's easy to talk about."

"It is okay, Adele, you can tell me anything. I promise.

I'm a good listener."

I study the motion of the lake for several more minutes before my mouth parts and words begin to flow between us. "Morgan, when Spencer died," I begin. "I was beyond depressed, I was suicidal."

"I can understand how difficult that must have been for you, Adele."

"Yes, but what you may not be able to understand is what I decided to do to cope with my pain."

"Go on."

I draw circles in the water with my feet and bite my bottom lip while I try to think of the right words, but there are no "right" words. Only the words that will explain to him what I've done, regardless of the consequences. I take a deep breath. "Morgan, a few weeks ago I drove to Utica, to a bar known as the Lounge to meet with a man by the name of Carl Nardone."

"Carl Nardone the gangster?" Morgan asks. "The one that was just recently shot?"

"Yes. So you've heard of him?"

"Yes," Morgan says as he drinks more coffee.

"I heard about him from, well, never mind about that. That's not important," I say.

"Okay, just tell me what you think is important."

"When I met with Carl, I handed him a very large sum of money in return for a service."

"How large of a sum and what kind of service?"

I lean back onto the palms of my hands and let my head fall backwards and stare up at the sky. "Ten thousand dollars and I ordered a hit."

"A hit? Adele, what are you talking about?"

"Morgan, I told you this wasn't going to be easy to tell, or hear. Do you want me to go on?"

"Yes, of course," Morgan says as he too leans back on the palms of his hands.

"I ordered a hit on myself."

Morgan sits up straight and turns his head back around to face me. "What? I don't understand."

I take another deep breath. "I paid Carl Nardone ten thousand dollars to have someone kill me. I was so depressed. Beyond depressed. I was ready to die."

"Adele, are you crazy? These people don't mess around."

"I know," I say. "That's why I'm telling you all of this now. I've changed my mind. I don't want to die. Not anymore."

"That's good."

"Right, but here's the thing. I drove back out to the Lounge to talk to Carl, to call it off, but as luck would have it that was the night he was killed. Morgan, I was there. Standing two feet away from him when he was shot."

"Are you kidding me?"

"I wish I were," I say as the memory of that night flashes in front of me. I can almost taste Carl's blood again. "But, I'm not kidding, I was there, but never able to talk to him before he was killed."

"Yes, but if he was killed then you're okay, right?"

"No. That's just the thing. The day I met with him he explained to me that it wouldn't be him doing the hit, it would be someone else. Someone I don't know. Carl would get twenty percent of the money while the hit man got the rest. So now I have no idea of knowing whether or not the message of my hit was ever delivered."

"But you're still here…"

"Well, that's the second part of this mess. When I met with Carl, I asked that the hit not happen until Labor Day weekend because I needed some time to get some things in order. I needed to sell my house, hire a new jewelry maker for the boutique, etcetera."

"So let me get this straight. Right now there could be a hit man out there scheduled to kill you sometime over Labor Day weekend and you, we, have no way of calling it off?"

"Bingo."

"Fuck."

"Right," I say and stand up and walk slowly back towards the cottage. I turn around to see if Morgan is following me.

He's not.

* * *

After I return to the cottage I get dressed and then busy myself for a few minutes folding up the blankets and sheets from our make-shift bed in the living room and tuck everything out of sight. When Morgan finally returns from the dock, I'm in the kitchen cooking breakfast. I'm not hungry, but I figure we should eat something before we leave today. This may be our last day together.

"Adele, we need to talk," Morgan says as he shuts the glass door and steps into the kitchen. I knew this was coming so I sit down at the table and prepare myself for the worst.

"I'm listening," I say as I cling tightly to my second cup of coffee.

"I've been outside thinking, and we need to go back to the Lounge and do some poking around. Maybe we can find some of Carl Nardone's business associates."

I stand up and look Morgan straight in the eye. "Do you mean you want to help me?"

"Of course I want to help you. Why wouldn't I?"

I throw my arms around his neck and hold him close. "Oh, Morgan, I thought for sure you'd be running for the hills over this. Thank you! Thank you so very much!"

Morgan continues to hold me, his arms around my hips. "Don't thank me yet, I haven't done anything."

"Yes, but at least you are willing to try," I say as I return to the stove and crack a few eggs into a pan.

"I'll try, that much I can promise you," Morgan says as he takes a seat at the table, still wrapped in his blanket.

"Do you want to get dressed before we eat?" I ask.

"No, thanks. All this talk about hit men and gangsters has made me really hungry," he says as he drops the blanket to the floor and sits at the table wearing nothing more than a smile. His eyes shine with the pure fire of a great purpose. "After we eat, we'll pack up and head towards Utica," he says.

"Great," I say as I cut into my eggs and exhale.

21.

It is shortly before noon when we pull into Utica. Most of the businesses downtown are either boarded up or closed for lunch with the exception of the Lounge where three motorcycles and two pickups are parked out front. Morgan pulls the car into the vacant lot across the street and we exchange long glances. I agree to let him do most of the talking once we get inside and to follow his lead. *It couldn't hurt.* So we step out into the sunshine, cross the street and enter the darkness of the Lounge.

Once inside, I look for the blood stains on the carpet next to the door. It looks as though someone has tried to erase them but to no great avail. I step over the dark blotches and look at Dixon, who is behind the bar. He recognizes me (or my drink) immediately. "Gin and tonic, two limes, you're back."

I nod but wait for Morgan to speak. Morgan bellies up to the bar and I take a seat beside him. "Hi, the name is Morgan."

"Glad to meet you, Morgan," Dixon says. "What are you drinking?"

"I'll take a draft, anything but a light," Morgan says and turns his head towards me.

"I'll have the usual, Dixon," I say. Stating his name serves as an introduction for Morgan.

Dixon pours our drinks and looks around the bar. "Quiet in here today," Dixon says. "Usually on a Saturday afternoon we'd have more people by now."

"Must be they've been scared away by the murder here the other night," Morgan says as he drops a fifty dollar bill from his wallet and pushes it across the bar.

"Maybe," Dixon says. "But the crowd here doesn't scare too easily," he adds as he takes the fifty and begins to make change.

"Keep the change, Dixon. I'd like to ask you a few questions."

"You a cop?"

Morgan laughs. "Do I look like a cop?"

"Can't tell these days," Dixon says with stone cold eyes still waiting for an answer.

"No, I'm not a cop. Just a concerned citizen is all."

"I see," Dixon says as he forgoes the change and shoves the fifty into his front pocket and pours himself a beer. "That will be an additional five bucks for the drinks, Morgan," Dixon says as he gives Morgan a look that he seems to understand. "What can I do for you two today?"

Morgan takes a sip of his beer and looks around the bar. "My friend here had some important business with Carl Nardone, but his untimely death has made it impossible for her to continue their conversation."

"I see," Dixon says as he too takes a sip of his beer. "Not sure I can help you with that, my friend."

"But you must see who Carl associates with," Morgan says as he presses the issue. "Anyone at all that may have knowledge of my friend's conversation with Nardone?"

Dixon's eyes are reduced to slits as he breathes in between his teeth and thinks for a minute. "There is one guy, goes by the name of Cleveland. He may be able to help you."

"Great," Morgan says as he shoots me a short smile. "Where can we find this Cleveland?"

"Hard to say, sometimes he comes in on the weekends. You might find him here later on tonight."

Morgan pulls a five dollar bill out of his pocket and hands it to Dixon. "That's for the drinks, man. Thanks. We'll be back later tonight."

"Cool, see you then." Dixon turns to ring up the drinks at the cash register while Morgan and I stand up and leave, my untouched drink rests on the bar.

When we get outside, I fist-bump Morgan. "That was amazing! Who knew you had such skills."

"Well, we still don't know if this Cleveland knows anything about you, but it's a start," Morgan says as he returns the fist-bump, and we walk together to the car. "Are you hungry?"

"A little."

"Me too, let's get something to eat and then go for a long walk along the river. After that we'll find something to do in this Godforsaken town until it's time to return to the Lounge."

"Sounds good, let's go."

22.

The Mohawk River flows through a portion of New York State from west to east and lies just north of Utica. Morgan and I arrive on the southern shoreline where we find kayaks for rent. The smell of the warm wind coming off the river pulls us in, and we quickly decide that this is what we will do today to occupy our time.

Although it is against the current, we plan to kayak west, towards Syracuse. On the return trip we will have the wind at our backs pulling us towards Utica. We'll go as far as Whitesboro and turn around. That will be about a five-hour trip, according to Clay, the man renting us the kayaks.

A stand is selling bottled water and snacks nearby so we load up with some provisions before shoving off. Clay warns us to bear to the right when we get to a point where we can either go left, straight or right. "When you see some fallen trees, again, bear to the right. And don't forget to stretch your legs every once and a while and take a few breaks along the way," Clay advises.

"Thanks, got it," I say as I step into my bright yellow kayak and hunker down.

"Let's have some fun," Morgan says as he gives my kayak a good push into the water and then jumps into his. We paddle against the current as hard as we can and head towards Whitesboro.

Less than ten minutes into the trip and we come across a pair of great blue herons in search of food along the rocky shoreline. Morgan is quick to point out the additional wildlife he sees along the way: mallards, blue jays, dragonflies, red-winged blackbirds, frogs and an occasional bass and tiny silver minnows swimming close to the bottom of the river. The river curves and winds for several miles and we are truly amazed by the natural beauty of Utica. Sadly, it's an area that is most likely being overlooked by the thousands that live here. At least, I am certain that the patrons that frequent the Lounge probably never see this part of Utica. Here is an oasis from their city lifestyle, right in their own backyards. I begin to wonder if Carl had ever embarked on a river kayaking trip, then remember about our intended meeting with Cleveland later tonight. I break the silence of our river talk and bring up the topic. "If we see Cleveland tonight, have you thought about what you're going to say to him?" I ask.

"Yes," Morgan says as he paddles up alongside my kayak and holds onto the side of it slowing us both down. "Let's take a break here," he says and I follow him to the northern shoreline. We easily climb out of our kayaks, rest beneath the shade of a giant sycamore tree and pull out our snacks; packages of string cheese with wheat crackers and two bottles of water.

"What are you going to say to him?" I ask as I rip into my cheese and tear it into long strips.

"Well," Morgan begins. "I'm going to ask him if he's ever heard your name. If he has, then we know he knows something. That's the best-case scenario we can hope for. In which case, I'll take it from there. But, if he doesn't know your name – and I'll read him as well as I can – then I'll ask him if there is anyone else that may know something about your and Carl's discussion."

I nod my head in agreement as I welcome the cool, bottled water against my scratchy throat. It's a hot day but soon I discover that even the heat cannot pierce the desires of the heart. The branches of the sycamore help keep the sun away from our flesh as we lie back onto the soft grasses where Morgan begins kissing me. The smell of wild honeysuckle mixed with the chirps, babbles and clucks of some ducks swimming nearby fills my senses as we undress under the cover of light shade and make love in the light of day until we fall asleep.

* * *

When I wake, the air feels warm and thick. The hot rays of the sun have found us once again as it begins its decent into the western sky. "Wake up, Morgan," I say as I get dressed and take a look around. There is not another soul in sight but there is a heavy scent hanging in the air like smoke. I stand up and search the horizon over Utica. We have traveled about five miles but I can still see the city limits and the smoke billowing in the sky above that general direction. Morgan dresses and stands up.

"Something is definitely on fire in the city," he says. "Let's get back there and find out what's happening."

"Right," I say as I climb back into my kayak and wait for Morgan to do the same. As expected, the current pulls us along, and we are back where we started in less than one hour.

Clay is standing on the shoreline waiting to pull us in. "I was starting to get worried about you two," he says as he pulls both kayaks onto the rocky shore but otherwise wastes little time telling us what he knows about the fire inside the city.

"Where about is it?" Morgan asks as we each remove our life jackets.

"Downtown, east of the college," Clay says as he stacks the kayaks up inside his shed. "I hope you're not heading that way. They've got the roads all blocked off in and out of the city. It's a five-alarmer."

"Jesus," Morgan says as he shoots a glance in my direction. "Looks like we're not going back to the Lounge tonight."

"The Lounge?" Clay asks. "That's on Sunset Street, isn't it?"

"Yes, it is," I answer.

Clay takes the life jackets from us and throws them into a red plastic bin resting beside the shed as he makes a snapping sound with his tongue and cheek. "That's not good. The fire is on Sunset Street," he says and then invites us into the shed to listen to his police scanner.

The scanner is buzzing with activity and we learn that the fire is centered around the intersection of Sunset and Newell, about three blocks from the Lounge. We can't be certain but the three of us figure that the Lounge has probably been spared. Morgan and I will have to wait until tomorrow morning to find out for sure. We thank Clay for the use of the scanner and the kayaks, and then ask him if he can recommend somewhere good to eat. Somewhere we can get to even with the fire downtown. "Do you like Greek food?" he asks.

"Love it," we both say.

"Then head over to Symeon's Restaurant, on the outskirts of town, on the west side. Best Greek food in three counties," he says and waves good-bye as he locks up his shed and calls it a night.

23.

On the last Sunday of June, Morgan and I rise from his bed and head once again towards Utica. The news reports out of Syracuse do not give enough detail, so we need to see for sure if the Lounge is still standing. And, if not, how can we go about finding Cleveland outside the familiar surroundings of the bar? Once we arrive downtown, the eerie quiet that has fallen over the city is disturbing. Utica, before the fire, was by no means the epicenter of the state, but it is even more depressing now that the fire has raged through its streets. Townspeople meet on the sidewalks and whisper their theories to one another regarding the cause of the fire. It has already been determined to have been arson, not surprisingly, but by whom? Three businesses, thriving businesses, have all been burned to the ground. The shoe store operated by a Jewish couple from Boston. A laundry mat located next door to the shoe store and operated by an Italian woman by the name of Lucia and, finally, a pawn shop owned and operated by the Vitale family, known to have ties to the old Buffalo Mafia. All gone. The shelled remains of the three structures are still smoldering as Morgan and I drive slowly past the wreckage with our windows down to survey the damage first hand. The smell of black soot and smoke permeates the air which is already humid and uncomfortable. It's devastating to look at, but we have no reason to believe that the Lounge, three blocks over, has been involved so we turn the car around and head back in the direction of Sunset Street.

And we are correct. The Lounge is still standing with the typical pickups and motorcycles parked out front. We decide to pay another visit. Maybe we'll get lucky and discover Cleveland is not a religious man either and, like us, has nowhere else to go on this sticky Sunday morning.

Inside, standing behind the bar is a woman we do not recognize. Apparently, even Dixon gets a day off. This woman appears to be about fifty-five years old. Stocky, black hair, without a touch of gray, and a cigarette perpetually suspended from her lips as she speaks. "What will you have?"

"We're looking for Cleveland," Morgan says. "Have you seen him around today?"

"Cleveland? This early, you must be joking! I don't think Cleveland's eyes have seen the light of day since 1992," she says and lets out a hardy laugh causing some cigarette ashes to fall onto the bar. "Try back later tonight," she says as she washes down the bar with a wet rag. "But come when it's good and dark if you have any chance of finding Cleveland around here." She laughs again as the dirty rag leaves wet circles on the far-from-clean bar.

"Thanks," Morgan says, and we escape the Lounge once again to step outside into the ungodly heat of the day. "Do you want to go swimming?" Morgan asks.

"Swimming? Really?"

"Yea, why not. We could head over to Sylvan Beach."

"I don't have a bathing suit with me," I say. "But I'd love to cool down and get out of this heat."

"Can you pick one up at Wal-Mart? I can swim in what I have on," Morgan says as he rubs his hands down the sides of his shorts.

"Sure, that will work," I say with a smile. Being around Morgan is so rejuvenating. He is four years older than I, but I would swear he was years younger. His enthusiasm for life is contagious and I only wish I had met him before I hired

Carl. *Oh, God, for oh so many reasons!*

After a quick stop at Wal-Mart, we are on the road again headed for Sylvan Beach on the east shore of Oneida Lake north of Syracuse. When we arrive, we discover it's, "Free Fishing Weekend" and the beaches are jammed packed with fisherman of all ages, sizes and sex. We walk a little north of the main beach and find a semi-secluded spot where we can be left alone to swim at our own leisure. Morgan lays a blanket out in the sand, and we plop ourselves down and begin to lather on sunscreen.

The sun is a giant blaze of gold suspended over the eastern hills as I gingerly make my way across the hot sand and approach the water's edge. The familiar crunch of dry pebbles feels warm against my feet and welcomes me into the shallow waters. Oneida is tranquil and still until a plopping sound of a fish breaks the surface and sends a widening ripple across the lake. I watch as a pair of dabbling ducks, swimming in the shallow water tip their tail feathers into the air and dip their beaks in search of food.

The quickening sensation of noise and motion as sailboats navigate their way south piques my interest. The eager wind greets the sails which snap to attention, billowing in the sky as they develop a delightfully low hum like whistling woodwinds. The water responds, rhythmically, as it slaps against the hulls. I close my eyes and linger for a while, getting lost in the harmony when Morgan suddenly thunders in behind me and runs into the lake and does a cannonball making a colossal splash. I smile knowing how Spencer would have loved Morgan. "Where have you been all my life, Morgan Spencer?" I whisper as he resurfaces and the water glistens off of his bare chest.

Morgan pretends to be some sort of sea creature and dives into the water and circles around my feet several times before he picks me up and throws me into the lake. I don't know whether to laugh or scream. The water is so cold but the coldness against my parched flesh feels good, and I am happy to finally be completely wet. I, too, dive into the water and do a handstand or two and remember what if feels like to be young and alive as the sun suddenly disappears behind a cloud. "Morgan, what if we don't find Cleveland?"

"Then we'll move to the south of France," Morgan declares, and I can't tell whether he is joking or not. I haven't completely figured out his sense of humor yet, but I assume he's joking, splash him with water and then it's on. We spend what seems like an eternity dunking and splashing each other in the face with the chilly water. I climb on top of Morgan's shoulders and do a spectacular dive into the lake, which he applauds. Soon we wrap our arms around each other in the shoulder-deep depths of the lake, and we kiss and we kiss and kiss some more.

When the time finally comes for us to return to Utica, we are exhausted and hungry, not to mention wet and covered with sand. "How about we drive back to my place, take a shower, get cleaned up and something to eat before heading back to Utica?" Morgan suggests.

"That's a great idea. I'd really like to wash this lake water off of my skin before getting changed back into my dry clothing."

"All right, we'll be there in about thirty minutes. Can you wait that long until you eat?"

I'm really hungry, but I don't want to seem too anxious so I take the safe route. "I can if you can," I say and wait for his decision.

"We better stop at McDonald's," he says with that boyish grin that I have grown to love, and I can already taste a quarter pound cheeseburger with extra mustard and onions as he pulls the Subaru onto the sand and does a quick doughnut as we exit the parking lot to leave Sylvan Beach in our wake.

* * *

The moment we reach Morgan's cottage, my cell phone rings. It's Orlando. "Hi, Orlando," I say as I step out of the car and brush some more sand from my calves.

"How's your weekend?" Orlando asks. "I hope I'm not disturbing you."

"No, not at all. We just got back from the lake and are about to get cleaned up. What's up?"

"I just wanted to tell you about Ellie Wilson, I think we should hire her."

"Really? She's that good?"

"Yes, she brought in some sample pieces of her work and they are amazing. Really. I know they'd sell."

When Orlando says something will sell then it's like money in the bank, but I decide I should at least meet her before I commit to a new hire. "Do you think you can ask her to come back out one day next week to meet with me?"

"I'm sure that won't be a problem, tomorrow?"

"Sure, tomorrow's great, if she's available. Anytime. I don't have anything specific scheduled."

"Okay, thanks Deli. I'll set it up. Enjoy the rest of your day," he says and I think I can hear him smiling.

"Thanks, Orlando. See you tomorrow," I say as I step inside the cottage. Morgan is busy tending to his many plants and I ask if I can jump into the shower first.

"It's all yours, babe," he says and it's the first time he's ever called me anything besides 'Adele.' I like the sound of it. As a matter of the fact, I like the feel and sound of everything when I'm with Morgan.

    I step into the shower and let the spray of the water run over my tanned flesh as I think about returning to the Lounge. I'm so tired of that shitty place, but I know we need to go back. It's the single most important task of my life right now. Ironic, I think, as Morgan steps into the shower and asks me to pass him the soap. We lather each other's body and linger in the mist until the water turns cold causing us to recoil. We then try to beat each other out of the shower as the relentless cold water beats down on top of us. Morgan wins, and I am left to reach under the cold spray and struggle to turn off the water. S*weet agony!* Morgan stands waiting for me with a warm bath towel spread open wide. Jokingly, he pats me dry a few times and then leaves me to get dressed in private. *Does it get any better than this?* I wonder as I dress and comb out my long hair.

    I join Morgan in the living room and find him singing and playing his guitar, a Train song, in an upbeat tempo as he smiles and dances around the room with me, and I am certain, it doesn't get any better than this.

    The time quickly disappears and it turns dark outside; time to drive back to Utica. I grab my bag from the sofa and announce I am ready when Morgan suggests I go home and get a good night sleep. He'll drive out to the bar alone and talk to Cleveland, if he can find him, and let me know later on what he finds out.

    "Really?" I ask.

    "Really," he says as he wraps his strong arms around me and walks me to the car. "Let's get you home, babe."

24.

The next morning I arrive at the boutique bright and early. A somber and breathless calm hangs over the shop as I open up the doors and think about Morgan meeting with Cleveland last night. I sense he was successful, and that they now hold a secret sweeter than the sea or sky can whisper - my life will be spared.

I open the safe below the cash register and find a cloth bag marked 'samples' and fish inside. I pull out a pair of delicate silver earrings perfect for everyday wear, two bracelets and one man's black onyx ring skillfully sculpted with an oak tree cut into the ebony stone and detailed shoulder embellishments on the side of three lions' heads. I know immediately I want the ring as a gift for Morgan, when the time is right. And then I know Orlando is right. If these are Ellie Wilson's pieces then we need to hire her, now, before someone else does. As I carefully tuck the jewelry back inside the bag, Orlando enters the shop looking just marvelous. He too, apparently, has been out in the sun this weekend and is looking completely relaxed and tanned. "Well hello, gorgeous," he says, giving me his best Barbra Streisand expression as he looks at me over the rim of his dark sun glasses. "It looks like you got some sun, too, Deli."

"Yes, sir. We went to Sylvan Beach."

"Sylvan Beach? I thought you were going to the Finger Lakes," Orlando says as he tucks his backpack underneath the counter.

"Oh, yea, we were going to but they messed up our reservation so we ended up staying at Morgan's cottage near Onondaga Lake and made some day trips."

"Ah huh," Orlando says as he raises his eyebrows. "I bet you two didn't get out of bed all weekend and that beautiful suntan of yours is from a bottle."

"Oh, stop it, Orlando. Would I lie to my besty?" *Yes, apparently I would.*

Orlando smiles and sits down behind the counter. "Did you find Ellie's samples?"

"Oh my goodness, yes! They are stunning. I want that onyx ring," I say as I turn on the computer.

"And what are you going to do with a man's ring? Oh, wait, I know, it's a gift for yours truly, right?" He says as he rests his chin on the back of his interlocked hands and gives me a Cheshire cat smile.

"Close, but I thought I might buy it for Morgan. But it's too soon, right?"

"Ah, duh! Yea, it's too soon Deli. Don't go scaring away the man!"

Then I think about Carl and the Lounge and Cleveland and think one little ring can't possible scare away Morgan. But Orlando is right, it's way too soon to be buying jewelry for each other. "Well, I might buy it anyway."

"So does this mean you think we should make Ellie an offer?"

"Yes, today. When she comes in. I was thinking we'll give her a hefty commission on the sale of her jewelry and a modest starting salary of $10 per hour. Does that sound okay to you?"

"How hefty of a commission?" Orlando asks.

"Forty percent."

"That sounds perfect," Orlando says. "I'm pretty sure she'll accept."

"What time is she coming in?"

"Two o'clock."

"Okay, great. It's typically pretty slow around here at that time so I'll sit down with her in the workshop. Thanks for setting it up."

"You're welcome," Orlando says as a young couple enters the shop. He is on his feet and at their service in no time flat.

When lunch time rolls around, my phone lights up with a message from Morgan.

Morgan: Can you meet me for lunch?

Me: Sure, where?

Morgan: Empire Brewing Company

Me: OK, see you in 10

When I walk into the restaurant, Morgan is waiting for me at a small table in the back of the room. He waves and I smile and savor the vision of him when a sudden, menacing desire to sit on his lap overcomes me. Pushing the thought from my mind, I lock eyes on him and walk past the bar to join him at his table. He is dressed in his old works clothes, covered in all colors of paint and grease with an old Syracuse cap worn backwards on top of his head and I'm not sure when he has ever looked more desirable. I know right then and there that I'm in love with him, for sure, but I take a seat in a chair and simply tell him how happy I am to see him again.

"Thanks, I'm happy to see you again, too," he says and gives me that ear-to-ear grin that makes me smile all over inside. "I went to the Lounge last night." Our conversation has suddenly turned serious, so I lean forward in my seat and ask him to tell me everything he knows.

"When I arrived last night, around ten, our old pal, Dixon was there. It was his night off but he was sitting at the bar having a beer so I joined him. After a few beers, he starts to tell me that the word around town is that someone from the Vitale family, most likely a punk named Tommy, shot Carl Nardone in a turf war. In retaliation, Nardone's people set the Vitale's pawn shop on fire which got out of control and took out the shoe store and laundry mat, too."

"That's terrible, but did you ever get to talk to Cleveland?"

"No, that's just the thing. According to Dixon, this turf war has taken on all sorts of priorities and implications and the heavies from Buffalo are coming to Utica, as we speak, to get to the bottom of the situation."

"I don't get it," I say, puzzled. "What does that have to do with me?"

"Adele, Cleveland is wrapped up in this tight so, as they say, he has bigger fish to fry right now."

I lean back in my chair and try to think what this all means for me. The waitress arrives to our table and I decline an entree but ask for a glass of water. "So does this mean we may never find Cleveland?"

"Maybe," Morgan says. "But, listen, I gave Dixon my card and asked him to give me a call if he sees Cleveland at the bar."

"That's good."

"I hope so," Morgan says and then adds, "The good news about all of this is that your hit may be long forgotten about with everything else that's going on with these people right now. As far as we know, no one even knows about you and all will be okay."

I take a long swallow of my water and stretch my hand to his. "Thanks, Morgan, for everything you've done. What do we do now?"

"I think we need to wait and hope that Dixon comes through and gives me a call."

Morgan finishes his cheeseburger in record time and we

kiss good-bye and head in opposite directions back to work. I pass by Cliff's office on the walk back and think about stepping in but what would I say? I decide against it and keep walking. *Could my hit really have been forgotten? And is this turf war really the best thing that could ever happen for me?*

    I'm not sure.

25.

I have Ellie Wilson's jewelry samples laid out on a piece of blue silk cloth on top of our display case when she arrives for her second interview. She is a girl of probably twenty-three or -four, no more. She has a warm, mocha colored complexion and shiny short black hair cut in a very stylish asymmetrical bob which completely covers her right eye. And it's a shame. Her eyes are quite possibly the most beautiful I have ever seen; large and fierce, and positively violet in color. I've heard of violet eyes but this is the first time I have ever witnessed them myself. I resist the temptation to tell her she should never cover them up and shake her hand instead. "Hi, Ellie. I'm Adele Hamilton, thank you for coming in today."

"Thank you for meeting with me," she says. Her smile is bright and genuine and I ask her to follow me back to the workshop. When we walk in, she looks around with wide-eyed excitement as she admires all of the various semi-precious stones and rocks, metals and tools. "What a great work space," she says and takes a seat on a stool. She is wearing a khaki skirt with a purple, short-sleeved blouse and when she crosses her legs I can see the tiniest hint of a tattoo on her upper thigh.

"Well, first of all, Ellie, I'm already a fan of your work. Especially that black onyx ring. Can you tell me what the inspiration behind it was?"

"Yes, of course. I made that ring in my senior year at Alfred, as an assignment. We were told to make something that represented someone in our life whom we loved and respected and I immediately thought of my grandfather,

Daryl White.

"Why so?"

"My grandfather worked on the railroad his entire life as a mechanic. It was a dirty, thankless job but what he loved more than anything else in the world was the woods, hence the oak tree carved into the stone."

"And the lions on the shoulder? What do they represent?"

"Oh, that, it's our sign. He, my mother and I are all born under the sign of Leo. The three lions represent us and our bond as a family."

"That's beautiful, Ellie. How'd you do on the assignment?"

"A plus," she says with a bright smile and I move on to my next question.

"Why would you like to work for a Bit of Silver, Ellie?"

She doesn't hesitate. "I would like to work here because of the reputation you have carved out for yourself in such a short time. You are famous at Alfred University and very well-known and respected right here in Syracuse where I live. When I heard you were interviewing for an intern I knew it was the job for me!"

I blush slightly at her high praise but decide to go right ahead and offer her the job. Heck, I'm thinking about adopting her. She is just so delightful. "Ellie, Orlando and I would like to offer you the job."

"Oh, thank you!" she squeals. "You won't be sorry, I promise."

"We'll pay you a starting salary of $10 per hour and give you forty percent commission on the sale of your pieces. We'd like you to begin as soon as possible and work approximately twenty hours a week. Does that sound appealing?"

"Yes, yes, thank you!" She says and jumps up from her stool and shakes my hand again. "Can I begin tomorrow?"

"You sure can. Now let's go give Orlando the good news."

Orlando is already standing outside the door to the workshop, waiting for us, holding a gold serving tray with three glasses of fizzling Champagne. "Is this too much?" he asks as Ellie and I laugh and I assure him it is not. We raise our glasses high into the air and toast to the future success of a Bit of Silver and close the shop for the day.

26.

On the first day of July, I wake and suddenly realize I need to start looking for a new place to live. *If* I should live. And the closing on my house is next month so I need to have something lined up soon, just in case. I decide the best person to call, once again, is Barbara Evans. "Hi, Barbara, it's Adele."

"Hi, Adele, how is everything? Are you busy packing?" I look around the house and realize this is something else I haven't even begun to think about. I need to pack, soon.

"Well, not exactly," I say. "But I'm getting ready to. But, I need to find a new apartment. Can you help me with this?"

"Sure, whereabouts?"

"Somewhere in Armory Square, near the boutique. It would be nice to be able to walk to work, if possible."

"I have a lot of listings in Armory Square. When would you like to take a look at a few?"

"How about tonight, around six? We could meet at my boutique. You know where it's located, don't you?"

"Sure, I know it. I'll be there at six."

"Okay, thanks, Barbara. Bye."

After getting showered and dressed, I decide to take a drive out to see Mom before going into work. Orlando and Ellie will both already be at the shop, so I have even more leisure time now, and I'm beginning to really like it. Ellie has required very little training, if any at all, and we have already sold one of her pieces, a silver bracelet. She is busy now working on more items that look very promising. Orlando and I pour over her sketches every morning and delight in her imagination and pulse on what's "hot" right now. It was one of the smartest things we ever did, hiring Ellie.

When I pull up to Mom's house, there is a car in the driveway that I don't recognize. I hesitate, briefly, but decide it's probably just one of her girlfriends from the gym. I walk in through the back door, as always, and yell for Mom as I pour myself a cup of coffee from the pot on the stove. She doesn't answer. I take a sip of my coffee and throw a glass of water on the neglected fern resting on the window sill and think about Morgan. He would flip if he knew Mom's talent for killing plants.

"Mom?" I yell through the house until she finally appears, dressed in her bathrobe and looking a little startled. "Hey, there you are. Where's your walker?"

"Oh, that stupid thing. Don't need it anymore. I'm fine. I've been working out at the gym again and my physical therapist told me to use it as needed. And I don't need it. Adele, what are you doing here so early?"

"We hired a new jewelry maker at the boutique so I don't have to rush in anymore. I thought I'd stop in and have a cup of coffee with you."

"Well, sweetheart, I really wish you would have called first," she says as Cliff emerges from her bedroom dressed in his bathrobe, too. I turn to leave but Mom calls for me to stay. "Adele, please, sit and talk with us for a while, won't your please?"

"It looks like you're busy, Mom," I say as I turn to leave. I'm not exactly sure why I'm so angry but I am mad as a wet cat on a stormy night and all I want to do is get the hell out of this house. "I'll call you later," I say and I leave the same way I came in, through the back door.

As I drive to work, I soon calm down and realize that I

have overreacted. Mom deserves to be happy and if Cliff makes her happy then, well, that's great. *Who the hell am I to judge?* I decide to give Mom a call as soon as I arrive at the boutique and apologize for my bad behavior. Maybe she and Cliff and Morgan and I can have dinner together sometime. *This is a good thing, Adele,* I tell myself as I continue to drive and turn on the radio.

The morning news comes on and I listen intently as the announcer informs that another person is currently being held for questioning by the Syracuse Police for the disappearance of Valerie Dunne.

I have so many thoughts running through my mind as I walk across the square and enter the boutique where, waiting for me inside, are Orlando, Ellie and two Syracuse Police Detectives.

* * *

I hear the two detectives introduce themselves and explain to me that they are here to ask me a few questions about Morgan Spencer. I feel numb as a pale succession of day's flashes before my eyes. I lead them back to the workshop and offer them each a chair.

Both men remain standing.

They appear to be about the same age, mid-forties, I'd guess. Detective Ganzon, the shorter or the two, pulls out his business card and hands it to me and I feel like I already know the drill. Later, when he leaves, he'll ask me to call him if I can think of anything more but I have no idea why they are here in the first place. I take a seat.

"Ms. Hamilton," Detective Ganzon begins. "How long have you known Morgan Spencer?"

"For about three of four weeks," I say as I look away,

not prepared for this. I forget to maintain eye contact with him.

"How did you make his acquaintance?"

"Here, in the boutique," I say. "He came in looking for a graduation gift for his niece."

"Did he mention the niece's name to you by any chance?" Ganzon asks.

I search my memory and try to come up with the girl's name. "It was Waverly, I think."

"Okay, thank you," he says as he flips over a page in his notebook before continuing. "On Sunday, June 16th, did you have dinner with Mr. Spencer?"

"Yes," I say as I look over at the second detective. He too scribbles down some notes. "What's this all about?"

"We'll get to that," Ganzon says. "Where did you and Mr. Spencer have dinner?"

I can feel my cheeks turning bright red because obviously if they know I had dinner with Morgan that night then they probably know where, too. But I answer him. "At the Onondaga Yacht Club. I had the lamb."

"What time would you say the two of you left the restaurant?"

"I remember the sun just beginning to set over the lake but it wasn't quite dark yet. Probably around 7:30 or 8:00 p.m.," I say.

"And after dinner did you go anywhere else with Mr. Spencer that night?"

"No. He drove me back here, to pick up my car and then I drove home, alone. What's this all about?" I ask again.

But Ganzon presses on and ignores my question. "When you and Mr. Morgan where at the Yacht Club, did anything unusual occur that night?"

I know where this is going and I don't like it. I wonder if I need an attorney or if I'm obligated to keep answering his questions. My head begins to pound and my ears begin to ring when I think I may pass out. I ask if I can get myself a glass of water.

"Detective Williams will get you a glass of water," Ganzon says as he motions to the water cooler in the corner of the room and gestures with his hand to Detective Williams.

After I take a sip of the water I ask Detective Ganzon to repeat his last question. "Yes, of course, I'll repeat the question," he says. "When you and Mr. Morgan where at the Yacht Club having dinner on the night of June 16th, did anything out of the ordinary occur?"

"Yes. Our waitress spilled a tray of drinks in my lap."

"That must have been very unpleasant." He smiles.

"Yes, it was," I say as I straighten my spine.

And then Detective Ganzon pulls out a picture of Valerie Dunne and I feel myself begin to tremble. "Do you recognize the woman in this photograph?"

"Yes. That's Valerie Dunne, our waitress at the club that night." I stand up. "I need to insist now that you tell me what this is all about."

"Ms. Hamilton, please sit down. We are investigating the disappearance of Valerie Dunne, and we have identified Morgan Spencer as a person of interest. We simply need to ask you a few questions in order to rule him out as a suspect."

"Did his crazy sister talk to you? If so, I can assure you, she doesn't have any idea what she's talking about. She's nuts!"

Ganzon and Williams do not say a word to me but I feel I have made my point. They both close their notebooks and turn around to leave and, as expected, Detective Ganzon asks me to give him a call if there is anything more I can think of that they might consider useful information. "Anything at all," he says.

"Where is Morgan now?" I ask.

"We have him downtown, at the station."

"Has he been arrested?"

"No," Ganzon says and he and Detective Williams leave the boutique and wish me a good day.

After the detectives leave I go into the ladies room and try to pull myself together. My hands are shaking and my ears are still ringing, and I don't know what to believe. *Morgan is being detained because he possibly had something to do with Valerie's disappearance?* I consider all of the possibilities when Orlando taps on the door and asks me if I'm okay.

"Yes, I'm fine," I lie. "I'll be right out."

When I emerge from the ladies room, five minutes later, Orlando is waiting for me in the workshop. He closes the door and asks me to sit down. "Deli, what's going on? That's two sets of police detectives that been out here to talk to you. As your friend, and your business partner, I deserve to know the truth."

And he is right. My life has become unrecognizable and a complete mystery, even to me. But I cannot, will not, tell Orlando about the hit man. He would never understand and it would only worry him to death. I take a seat next to him and tell him why the Syracuse Police were just here to see me.

"Oh my God, Deli, do you think Morgan killed that poor girl?" Orlando asks.

"I don't know what to think, Orlando. The Morgan I know is sweet, kind; loving and completely harmless. It couldn't be true. It's got to all be a big misunderstanding."

"What are you going to do?"

"I don't know. Do you think I should go down to the police station and see him?"

"No. Absolutely not," Orlando says as he stands up and put his hands on his hips. "I'm not even sure you should ever see him again, Deli. You just met the guy and who knows, he could be a murderer!"

I think about those words and know in my heart that it cannot be true. The Morgan I know wouldn't hurt a fly.

"Deli? What are you going to do?"

"I'm not sure." I say, but secretly decide I will drive by Morgan's place later on tonight and hear his side of the story. I feel that I owe him that much.

27.

As Orlando and I are getting ready to close the boutique for the day, I am initially surprised when Barbara Evans walks through the front door until I remember I have an appointment with her to look at a few apartments. I would like nothing more than to get out of it but I feel I cannot, she drove all the way out here just to see me.

"Hi Barbara. I'll be ready to leave in just a few minutes," I say as she enters the boutique. "Barbara, I don't think you have ever met my business partner, Orlando Ramos."

"No, I don't think I have," Barbara says as she and Orlando shake hands. "Nice to meet you, Orlando."

"Orlando, Barbara is my realtor. She is going to show me some apartments here in Armory Square tonight."

"Oh, how wonderful! Nice to meet you, Barbara. Be sure to find something nice for our Deli. She deserves the best," Orlando says as he grabs his backpack and gives me a wink. "Good-night, ladies."

"Good-night," I say. "See you tomorrow."

"Nice to meet you, Barbara," Orlando says as he walks outside and into the square.

Barbara browses the boutique for a few minutes while I shut down the computer and turn off the lights. Five minutes later I am ready, and we walk together to the first apartment on her list. Only a ten-minute walk from the boutique, and located in the heart of downtown Syracuse, it's a two bedroom loft that overlooks the square. Inside, crown moldings, alabaster sconces and brand new hardwood floors accentuate the luxury of the apartment. "Barbara, this beautiful," I say as I walk to the kitchen window and look down over the square and rub my hand over the granite counter tops.

"I thought you'd like it," Barbara says. "It's available September 1st."

"That's Labor Day weekend, isn't it?" I ask.

"Yes, I think so," Barbara says as she opens her phone and checks the calendar. "Yes, September 1st is a Monday, Labor Day."

"Interesting," I say.

"Interesting? How so?" Barbara asks.

"Nothing, never mind. If I take it, can I move in two weekends before to coincide with the date of the closing?"

"Yes, I'm sure that will be okay but I will have to confirm it with the management and get back to you."

"All right," I say. "I don't think I need to see any more apartments. This one is absolutely perfect. I'll take it."

Barbara takes a seat at the kitchen counter. "Okay then, let's do the paperwork right now, if you're sure?"

"Yes, this is perfect. Exactly what I was looking for," I say as we complete the paperwork, then walk back to the parking lot together and say good-night.

After leaving Barbara, I drive to Morgan's cottage. When I arrive I see his Subaru parked in the driveway so I know he is home, but I sit in the car and loiter for a while as I think about the fact that I feel like I now know two Morgans; the one that I have fallen in love with and the one that is being interrogated by the police for the disappearance of Valerie Dunne. After a few minutes, I yield to the inevitable and my faith in Morgan, get out of the car and walk up the cobblestone path leading to his front door.

I knock on the door and when he doesn't answer I knock again. When he still doesn't answer, I send him a text.

Me: I'm outside, please open the front door.

Morgan: What are you doing here?

Me: The police came by the boutique today. We need to talk.

Two anxious minutes later, Morgan finally opens the front door. His hair is disheveled and he is wearing only a pair of boxer shorts and smells of whiskey and cigarettes. "Come on in," he says and I can feel the hairs on the back of my neck stand up. I look around the cottage and everything seems normal so I take a step inside.

"Morgan, what's going on?" I say as I take a seat in a chair close to the door.

Morgan grabs the bottle of whiskey of the coffee table, pours another tumbler and then stumbles to the sofa. "The police think I killed Valerie Dunne so I thought I'd get drunk," he says. "Would you care to join me?"

"No, I don't," I say. "Do you think this was Maria's doing?"

"Yep."

"Did you tell the police about her?"

"Yep."

"Well then, that's good. Once they speak to her they will find out she's not reliable and you will be absolved."

"Maybe. But I have a better idea. Let's get your hit man to kill my sister and then we'll kill two birds with one stone, get it?" Morgan says as he falls back onto the sofa and erupts with laughter.

"You're drunk."

"Yes I am. And I intend to stay drunk for as long as possible."

"I can't talk to you like this," I say as I stand to leave. "Call me in the morning, when you sober up."

"You got it, sweetheart," Morgan says as a ridiculous grin stretches across his face.

I turn to leave when I remember Waverly, Morgan's niece, and the dragonfly bracelet. "Morgan, how old did you say Maria was?"

"Thirty-eight, same as me."

"Does she have any children?"

"No, thank God."

I open the front door and the warm breeze coming off the lake brushes against my cheeks. "Do you have any other siblings?" I ask, but Morgan has already passed out and does not answer. I close the door and walk down the path which leads to my car and drive away when Mom calls. "Hi, Mom."

"Hi, Adele. Are you still upset with me?"

I take a few minutes to remember this morning, it seems so long ago, and then realize I acted like a spoiled child. "No, Mom, I'm sorry. I owe you an apology. I'm not upset. I overreacted. I guess I was just shocked to see Cliff walking out from your bedroom."

"I wasn't sure whether or not you would approve," Mom says and I can hear the concern in her voice.

"Mom, I think it's a good thing, really. I'm happy for you. I've always liked Cliff."

"Oh, Adele, I'm so happy to hear you say that. Maybe we could all get together for dinner sometime."

"That would be great, Mom. But I really should hang up now. I'm driving."

"Oh, yes, of course, safety first. I'll talk to you tomorrow. I love you."

"I love you, too, Mom," I say and drive the remaining ten minutes to my house in silence.

28.

Three days later, I wake with a sense of dread on the morning of the Fourth of July when I hear my phone jingle to the tune of *Into the Mystic*. I roll over onto my side and lift my cell phone from the night stand. The picture I took of Morgan the day we went kayaking is smiling back at me but I let it go to message.

I get out of bed and walk into the kitchen. The sun pours into the room and warms my feet and I am reminded of Wellington. I miss the sight of him basking here, next to my feet, and the sound of his gentle purr. I take my cup of coffee out to the front porch and take a seat on the rocking chair. It's only eight o'clock in the morning but the heat is already oppressive; the air thick. I take a sip of my coffee when my phone goes off again. Reluctantly, I answer it on the third ring. "Hi, Morgan."

"Good morning," he says as he clears his throat. "I'm sorry about the last time we spoke. I was a little upset."

"You were drunk."

"Yes I was. Can I come over?" he asks but I'm really not sure if I want to see him again and let the silence linger. "Adele?"

"Now? You must be joking," I say. "I'm not dressed and I'm just drinking my first cup of coffee."

"That sounds perfect. If it's okay, I'll be right over."

An ebb and flow of thoughts trickle through my mind. I want to go back to the first day I met Carl and erase everything I've done. I want there not to be a Valerie Dunne, much less a missing one, and I want Morgan to be innocent of any crime other than stealing my heart.

"Adele?" he asks again.

"Okay, for a little while," I say and close my phone. *I need to ask him more about Waverly. Something is not adding up.*

As I sit and wait for Morgan, my neighbors, the McCormick family, are out for an early morning stroll. Owen, the oldest boy, is the same age as Spencer would be now and Jude, the youngest, is the spitting image of his lovely mother, Corin. "Hi, Mrs. Hamilton," Owen says with a warm and friendly smile as he waves to me.

"Good morning! Ready for the Fourth of July, are you?"

"Yes!" six-year-old Jude squeals. "We have sparklers!"

"You do? Good for you!" I say as I remember how much Spencer loved sparklers. "You be careful, now, okay Jude?"

"I will, Mrs. Hamilton," Jude says and then waves good-bye to me as his family continues walking down the street with their black lab, Oliver, in tow.

Morgan pulls up into the driveway ten minutes later. He is dressed in a pair of khaki shorts and a white tee-shirt and I can feel my pulse quicken. Just the sight of him makes me tingle. "Good morning," he says.

"Same to you," I say as he leans over and gives me a soft kiss on the cheek. "Would you like a cup of coffee?"

"No, thanks. I already had two cups," he says as he takes a seat on the porch swing. His strong legs kick off the porch floor and the swing sways forward and back.

"Morgan, I wanted to ask you about your niece, Waverly."

Morgan looks out at the road and then back towards me. "Okay, what about her?"

"I don't understand whose daughter she is. You said

Maria doesn't have any children. Do you have another sibling?"

"Oh, that," Morgan says as he shifts his weight uncomfortably in the swing. "I can see how you would be confused. Waverly is actually my college roommate's daughter. Kevin. We went to SUNY Cortland together. Waverly calls me Uncle Morgan and I've become accustomed to referring to her as my niece."

"Oh. Do they live around here?"

"No. They live in Buffalo, where Kevin is originally from."

"Did she like the bracelet?"

"Yes, she did. She called to thank me and sounded very excited about it."

"That's good, I'm glad she liked it."

Morgan looks back out into the road and I can sense the tension between us. *What do I say?* I continue to wonder when Morgan finally breaks the silence. "So, about the police investigation. You don't think I had anything to do with Valerie's disappearance, do you?"

I hesitate.

"Adele?"

"No, of course not," I say, finally. "But where does it stand with the police?"

"I don't know. I told them about Maria and her deranged thinking and according to my father there were two detectives out to the house looking for her but she apparently has left town."

"Do you think Maria has anything to do with Valerie's disappearance?"

Morgan stretches his arms straight out in front of him and shifts his weight in the swing once again. "I don't know. I don't think so, but who's to say? She has been known to do some pretty crazy things."

"Like killing my cat?" I ask.

"We don't know that Maria killed your cat but there was this one time when she striped down naked in December and waded in the Onondaga Lake in order to cleanse her soul," Morgan began. "She got frost bite really bad and almost lost a couple of her toes."

"That's terrible but it's not exactly what I was thinking."

"You're right. Besides, I know my sister. She's as crazy as a loon but I don't think she's capable of kidnapping anyone."

"When can I meet her?"

Morgan looks out into the road. "You want to meet her?"

"Sure, why not?" I ask. "I've already met her, sort of. I'd like to make it official."

Morgan is silent for a moment, then says, "Sure, okay, I'll set something up."

"Great," I say as the McCormick family walks past my house once again on their way back home, licking ice cream cones. I smile at them and return my attention to Morgan. "By the way, did I tell you I sold my house?"

"No, really? So soon?"

"I'm going to rent an apartment in Armory Square. I'm scheduled to move in two weekends before Labor Day on August 15th. Are you busy that weekend?"

"I am at your service," Morgan jokes. "What time do you need me here?"

"Well, assuming I'm still alive I could use your help on Saturday. Say around eight in the morning?"

"You *will* be alive and you've got it," Morgan says as he stands. "I'll be here at 8:00 a.m."

"Are you leaving?"

"Yes, I'm going to head back out to the Lounge, to see if Cleveland is around."

"Should I come?" I ask.

"No, I don't think so. I'll give you a call if I find him," he says as he leans down and kisses me once more before turning to leave.

"Thanks, Morgan, I appreciate everything you're doing to help me," I say as he flashes his tender smile and jumps into his car and pulls away.

After finishing my coffee I decide to start packing, beginning with Spencer's room. I gently open his bedroom door and peek inside. Everything is untouched since the day he died. A jar of peppermints, his favorite, rests on the desk beside his bed. His Wii game is still plugged in, waiting for us to play Super Mario Brothers together again. And Wellington II, his stuffed cat, lies on top of his giant blue pillow; the one he used to prop himself up on when he was too weak to sit up on his own. A tidal wave of despair sweeps over me. I lie down on Spencer's bed and roll over to one side. While hugging Wellington II, I smell the lingering sweetness of Spencer – peppermints mixed with cherry juice. And then, as if by magic, Spencer is still lying here next to me, crunching his peppermints and telling me not to worry. "I'll be fine, Mom, you'll see," I hear him say as juice and slivers of peppermint trickle out of the corner of his mouth and onto the fuzzy gray cat. I think about death itself and begin to fall back into the same sense of dread that I felt the first time I entered the Lounge and met with Carl. My mind crashes in around me as another memory of Spencer rolls down my cheek. I hug Wellington II closer and bury my face into its stomach and breathe Spencer in as deeply as I can and wonder how my life will ever be the same without my little boy to love.

29.

    The Fourth of July celebration in town is a family affair and I struggle with my decision whether or not to attend. One year ago, Lonnie, Spencer and I all went to see the fireworks in Liverpool and had a wonderful time. Spencer's cancer was in remission so we rented a bicycle built for three and road it through the park before the fireworks began. Spencer road up front and was thrilled to lead the way. This year, I'm afraid, the celebration will not be anything quite as glorious. But finally, with the last box packed and the house cleaned, I decide to jump into the shower and take a chance on a little fun.
    When I arrive, the shoreline of Onondaga Lake is packed with people. Children fly Frizbees and twirl glow sticks above their heads while the local high school band, the Warriors, march along the main trail as groves of police officers direct traffic. After parking my car, I settle on a spot next to a very large sycamore tree and spread out my Alfred U purple and gold checkered blanket. The air is still warm, and it is a crystal clear night, perfect for viewing the fireworks that are scheduled to begin at dusk.
    As I lean against the massive tree, I spot Morgan's parents, Forrest and Sylvia, walking across the park in my direction carrying a small picnic basket and a blanket of their own. Naturally, I wave to them but to my surprise they decide to join me. "Where's Morgan tonight?" Forrest asks as Sylvia stands stone-faced.
    "I don't know," I say. "He did stop by my house this morning as I was having my coffee but I haven't seen nor heard from him since."

"Do you mind if we sit down?" Forrest asks. "We have Chardonnay, Pecorino Romano and some tasty crackers."

I look up at him and then Sylvia, who seems unaware of Forrest's request to join me, but I don't care. "Certainly," I say. "Please do."

Duty bound, Sylvia spreads out their blanket a few feet away from mine and reluctantly sits down. "So, Adele, I understand you've recently sold your house?" Sylvia says, breaking her silence as she pours some wine into three paper cups.

"Yes, how did you know?" I ask, quite surprised.

"I play tennis with Barbara Evans," she explains.

"Oh, I see," I say.

"Yes, that devil woman beats me every game!" Sylvia says as she sips her wine and smiles for the first time tonight. "So did Morgan mention what he was up to today?"

"No, he didn't," I say although I know he was headed towards Utica in search of Cleveland but this is not information I intend to share with them, ever. "Do you think he'll show up here?"

"Doubtful," Forrest replies. "Morgan's not one of fireworks. Besides, he can watch them from his front yard if he has the notion."

"I wasn't aware he didn't care for fireworks. That's odd. Why not?" I ask.

"Because of the car crash," Sylvia says, coldly.

"Do you mean the crash that killed his wife, Gloria? I'm afraid I do not know too much about that; only that she died ten years ago."

Forrest and Sylvia exchange long glances. "And their daughter, too. Didn't Morgan tell you about his daughter?"

I balance my cup of wine between my knees and sit up straight. "His daughter?" I ask. "He has a daughter?"

"He did have one," says Sylvia. "But she died, too, along with Gloria.

Forrest bows his head and I wonder why Morgan left out this all-important detail. But, I, of all people can understand how the death of a child can affect a person. Gingerly, I press on. "What exactly happened?"

Sylvia takes a deep breath and seems to ponder on a cauldron of thoughts as Forrest lies down flat on his back and looks up to the sky. The fireworks begin to burst over the lake. I sense I should set aside my curiosity, but I cannot. "So, what happened? Can you tell me?" I ask again.

"It was ten years ago tonight," Sylvia begins. "The Fourth of July, 2004. Morgan and Gloria had just picked up the baby from our house. I call her the 'baby' but the truth is she was four years old at the time. Anyway, they were headed this way to watch the fireworks after a day spent on their boat enjoying a barbeque together. They intended to come here, of all places, to watch the fireworks together," she says and she, too, now bows her head. "Morgan had been drinking all day so Gloria drove. Something that Morgan still blames himself for today. It was a tractor trailer with a driver pulling an all-niter for three straight nights. After leaving our house, when Gloria turned onto the exit for the park, the tractor trailer didn't stop and smashed into them. Head on."

I let out a gasp and cover my mouth.

"Morgan, the only one not wearing a seat belt," she continues, "was thrown from the car but, miraculously, landed in some foliage on the side of the road and managed to survive. On a broken leg, he hobbled in the direction of the car but by then it, and the eighteen-wheeler, suddenly burst into flames, kicking him backwards onto the ground. Because of the fireworks nearby, the police and ambulance squad were on the scene within minutes but it was too late. Both Gloria and the baby died."

I, too, now lie down on my back and look up at the fireworks. "Poor Morgan, I had no idea..."

"I'm sure you didn't," Sylvia adds as she takes another sip of her wine and leans back against the tree.

"What was his daughter's name?" I ask.

In unison, they both respond. "Waverly."

"Waverly?" I ask to be certain I heard them correctly.

"Yes."

The outdoors seems to close in all around me but I ask, "How old would Waverly be today?"

"Fourteen," Sylvia says.

I close my eyes and fight back the tears; *she would have been graduating from middle school.*

* * *

After the fireworks end I decide to drive out to Morgan's cottage and tell him I understand. Christ, there have been many times when I think I can still hear Spencer so why not buy him presents, too, for milestones he can no longer achieve? Fourteen would be the age to be finishing up middle school so I know that the dragonfly bracelet was for his deceased daughter, Waverly. *Poor Morgan.* I want to snap my fingers and take us back to a time when both of our lives made sense; back before we met, before our children had died.

When I arrive, the cottage is dark, but I can hear music coming from deep within. As I approach the cobblestone path leading to the front door, I suddenly feel like an outsider and stop dead in my tracks. I do not hear Morgan's guitar, only keyboard music so I figure he has company;

probably one of the guys he jams with from time to time. Anything, I think, to take his mind off of the events of ten years ago tonight and the death of his family. When I finally take another step forward and onto the front stoop I find the door ajar just as the wind picks up outside, blowing in hard, off of the lake. Suddenly, I'm not sure if I should take another step until I hear the music growing more intense, like a battle cry. I recognize the classic melody immediately, Mozart's Requiem for a Dream, and know I need to get to him. *He needs me.* I feel goose bumps rise and I hesitate again, briefly, as the music grows even more powerful. *Not this, Morgan, not this one,* I think when finally I get up my nerve and barge right in.

Once inside, I look around the cottage but it is still very dark. There is one dim light at the far end of the room where I begin to make out the shape of a woman crouched over a black glittering keyboard. With only a candle by her side, I recognize her signature flaming red hair falling wildly in front of her face. The haunting melody bursts across the room as she turns to face me; her eyes glaze over me as she pounds out Mozart's death march. Her stare turns deadly as she recognizes me.

In my panic I utter a feeble cry, like a lamb to slaughter, and turn abruptly and run from the cottage; keeping pace with my pounding heart until I reach my car but Maria is following me, keeping steady pace with my stride. I manage to jump inside of my car but Maria reaches me before I can close the door and suddenly takes a hold of my long hair, relentlessly pulling me towards her. I fight against her rage and manage to close the door. "Adele, stop, listen to me," she screams. If only I could turn the key, push in the clutch, get the car in gear when, finally, Maria's powerful grip is no longer a match for the car's stronger engine. I step on the gas and let go of the clutch. Hands, legs and body still trembling as I drive away. But I can still hear her shouting to me, "Come back, Adele, come back!" But I keep driving with no intention of turning around. *Where is Morgan?*

My tears continue to blind me as I drive – in excess of eighty miles per hour at times – heading straight towards the Spencer's farm. *I need answers!* I take the sharp bends at way too high a speed and blast down the tree-lined driveway, repeatedly honking my horn. I *want* to wake them up! I *need* to wake them up! I jump from my car and run to their front door where I pound both of my trembling fists until Forrest finally answers. "Adele, what are you..."

I push past him before he has a chance to finish. "I've just come from Morgan's cottage," I yell. "Tell me everything! What is going on with Maria?!"

If he answers, I don't hear it as I collapse into his arms.

30.

When I come to, I am lying on the sofa in the parlor next to the piano and Forrest, Sylvia and Morgan are by my side. There is an ice pack on my head; which is now throbbing, and my shoes have been removed. It is after midnight and I can hear rain drops bullet the eight foot windows of the spacious room. "Did I pass out?" I mumble.

"Yes," Forrest says. "Right after you asked me about Maria."

Sylvia takes a seat at the piano and crosses her arms across her chest. "I'm not sure we should tell her about Maria. She won't understand and besides, it's a family matter."

"Don't be ridiculous, Mother. I think she deserves to know the truth about Maria. I know that I, for one, am sick of her showing up at my place all of the time, that's why I came here tonight." Morgan says as he walks to one of the tall windows and lifts up the shade and stares out into the dreary night. "I'm going to tell her. Everything."

Sylvia storms over to the dry bar and pours herself a tall glass of vodka.

Ignoring Sylvia, Forrest returns his attention back to me. "How are you feeling, Adele? Would you like some aspirin?"

"No, thank you. I think I'll be all right with just the ice pack, but please, Morgan, tell me about Maria. She frightens me."

"What happened?" Morgan asks.

I tell them about the night's events and Forrest takes a seat in a comfortable leather chair flanking the fireplace and crosses his legs. He removes his pipe, a small cherry wooden bowl with a long stem, from his sweater pocket and begins to pack it. After he is satisfied, he takes a couple of hardy puffs, settles in and begins to speak as Sylvia takes a seat at the piano. "After the tragedy," he begins, "Maria was devastated. She blamed herself for not being here that day and therefore not being able to drive when Morgan could not."

"But that doesn't make any sense," I say. "Why would Maria feel responsible?"

Morgan takes a seat in the chair next to me closest to the sofa. "Because, Adele, it's what I tried to explain to you before. Maria is sick, she's schizophrenic, and most everything she does and thinks doesn't make sense. Due to her illness, she twists reality around in her head to the point where it's very difficult for us to understand or predict what she is going to do or say next. She has even told Mother that I killed Gloria and Waverly."

"I don't think I understand," I say. "How could she possibly think that? It was a car accident, right?"

"Right," they all say.

"Then I'm really confused," I say as my head continues to pound.

Forrest takes over the conversation. "It wasn't until Maria went off to Utica College and had…"

"Wait, Maria went to college in Utica?" I ask.

"Yes," Forrest continues. "She was enrolled in their nursing program. But, sadly, it was not to be. It was there that she had her first psychotic break, and we got the diagnosis of schizophrenia. Actually, that's not exactly true. The actual diagnosis is call schizoaffective disorder."

"What does that mean?" I ask.

"It means that our poor Maria is suffering from not only

schizophrenia but bi-polar disorder, too."

"So she has mood swings," Morgan interjects. "And most typically when she becomes manic she launches into a full psychotic episode as well."

"Do you think that is what was going on tonight when I ran into her?"

"Yes, most definitely," Forrest says. "Tonight is the ten year anniversary of Gloria and Waverly's death and this upsets Maria, terribly."

I glance up at Morgan. "How are you holding up?"

"I'm doing fine, it's just that this is hard enough without Maria adding to it," he says. "Mother told me that she explained everything to you about the night Gloria and Waverly died. I'm so sorry I lied to you about the bracelet. I guess I have my quirks, too," he says as he looks down at the floor. "I wanted to meet you so badly. I had seen you once before coming out of a Bit of Silver and once I realized you worked there I came up with the idea of ordering the bracelet for Waverly. She would have liked it," he says as his voice trails off and he looks down at the floor once again.

"I understand," I say. "But why did you feel you needed to lie?"

"I didn't want you thinking I was ordering a bracelet for another woman or something like that," he says and I smile. "It was stupid."

I remove the ice pack from my forehead and sit up. Thunder and lightning now cracks outside and casts long shadows upon the walls. My head is still pounding but I do not let on. Instead I walk to the bar and help myself to a drink, then resume my seat on the sofa. None of this about Maria is making any sense to me. I sit down, press the ice pack back into my right temple and take a sip of my drink.

"Morgan, is Maria dangerous?"

"I think she can be," Morgan says. "As a matter of fact, I think she may have killed your cat."

Sylvia looks away in disgust and bangs out Middle C on the piano as I gasp and place my hand over my mouth.

"You think she broke into my house?"

"Yes," Morgan says. "I think she was trying to send you a message."

"What kind of message?" I ask, trembling inside.

"To stay away from Morgan," Forrest says. "This is a big issue with Maria which is why she was pestering Valerie Dunne. She doesn't think anyone is good enough for her Morgan."

"This is sick," I say as I look up at Morgan once again. "How can you live like this?"

"It's not easy," he says, "which is why I usually don't date, at least not after the whole Valerie incident."

Forrest clears his throat, takes another puff from his pipe and crosses his arms across his chest.

"What exactly happened with Valerie?" I ask.

Morgan shifts his weight in his seat as Sylvia shakes her head 'no' but Morgan continues. "Maria kept sending Valerie threatening letters and stopping by the Yacht Club to pester her. Valerie just couldn't take it. She was so young."

"I don't blame her," Forrest says. "It would be difficult for anyone to take that type of harassment much less understand it."

"Well, I'm trying to," I say, "but, I admit, it's difficult."

"I told you she wouldn't understand," Sylvia sneers. "You've gone too far, Morgan, stop it. Stop it now!"

"Be quiet, Sylvia," Forrest says and then ignores his wife once again. His keen eyes are alert and caring. "What part don't you understand, Adele?"

I roll a chunk of ice around in my mouth, think before I speak and then I go for it. "Does anyone here think that Maria may have had something to do with Valerie's disappearance?"

Morgan kneels down at my side. "Adele, we're not sure."

I once again remove the ice pack from my temple and stand up. This is unbelievable, and I worry that I have gotten in too deep. I don't want to hear anymore.

"Do you understand?" Morgan asks.

"Yes, I think so, but what's being done about this? Have you gone to the police?"

"No, we haven't," Forrest says. "Maria is still part of this family. Morgan told them that Maria didn't approve of his relationship with Valerie, but we're not sure what the police made of that information, if anything at all."

I swallow the rest of my gin and tonic, set down my glass and try to shut my mouth, but I can't help myself, I'm in too deep. "What about Valerie's family? Don't they matter to any of you? It seems obvious to me that Maria is the killer. We should tell the police!"

"But we don't know for sure, Adele, and neither do you. It's just a hunch," Morgan says.

I walk to the piano where the picture of Maria rests, lift it into my hands and resume my seat on the sofa. As I stare into her eyes, I take a good look around the grand room and collect my thoughts. Wealth drips from every leather bound book, crystal chandelier and Persian rug. This family could afford a good attorney for Maria. They should turn her in; tell the police about the threats made to Valerie in the past. I brush the plush fabric of the sofa with the back of my hand and fluff the silk pillow behind my head. I think about the first time I met Morgan and the same affection I have felt for him all along resurfaces. It suddenly becomes completely clear to me what I need to do. "So where do we go from here?" I ask.

Sylvia whirls around to face me, mouth agape. "You mean you're not ready to run to the police?"

"No, of course not. I kind of like your son, Sylvia," I say as I smile fondly at Morgan.

"Thank you," Morgan says as Sylvia looks away, trying to hide her tears.

There is a long pause before any of us speaks until finally Forrest stands and breaks the silence. "Well, I think we've all had enough talk for one night. Morgan, please show Adele to the guest room."

"Yes, of course," Morgan says. "Are you ready for some sleep, Adele?"

"If I can sleep," I say as we say good night to Forrest and Sylvia and walk upstairs together. When we reach the top of the steps I turn and ask him, "Do your parents think we should sleep separately?"

"I don't care if they do," Morgan says as he takes me into his arms. "I'm not letting you out of my site tonight."

* * *

Five hours later, I wake to the sun splashing through the open window and streaking across the bedroom floor. I reach for Morgan's warmth but he is gone and his side of the bed has already been turned up.

I stand and walk to the window where the heavy scent of yellow roses transports me back to when I was a child in my Grandmother's garden. Sylvia suddenly enters the room, unannounced, breaking me from my memory. Moving gracefully and dressed in chartreuse-colored silk lounging pajamas, she carries a silver tray in her hands with a complete breakfast set atop: a glass of freshly-squeezed orange juice, one egg, two slices of wheat toast, a cup of black coffee and two aspirins. The coffee is rich and flavorful and the egg is perfectly-pouched. "This is wonderful, Sylvia, thank you." I sip my coffee and bite into a piece of toast.

She bows her head in thanks and adds, "Adele, about last night. I want to apologize for my rude behavior. I guess I get a little over-protective of Maria and her privacy. She was such a happy child. I hope you understand."

"Yes, of course. I understand completely. I had a son once..."

"Yes, I know. I heard about your Spencer, from both Morgan and Barbara Evans. I'm so sorry for your loss. He was much too young to be taken away from you so soon."

"Thank you, Sylvia. It has been very difficult for me."

"I'm sure it has," Sylvia says. "It's difficult for me, too, for all of us, dealing with Maria and her illness but at least we still have her with us. I don't know if I could survive the death of one of my children."

I lay my hand over hers and give it a gentle squeeze. "It's not easy, but we learn to deal with what God give us, right?"

"Yes, I suppose you are right," Sylvia says as she takes a bite of my other slice of toast and walks out of the room leaving me alone to eat my breakfast in peace.

Later, the early morning sun continues its slow creep across the tree-lined drive leading from the Spencer's farm as Morgan and I jump into our separate cars and wave goodbye to Forrest and Sylvia.

As I drive, I allow my spirit to roam in the clouds in

search of answers. In a life suddenly saturated with so many disasters, I am surprised to learn that my immediate feeling regarding Maria is one of relief. At least now I know what I am dealing with.

31.

As I pull into my driveway my cell phone jingles with a text.

Morgan: I'm going to head out to the Lounge again and see if I can finally meet the elusive Cleveland.

Me: Okay, can you come over later on tonight?

Morgan: Yes, planning on it.

Me: Thanks.

I throw my phone back into my bag and walk into the house. As I busy myself sorting through some old clothing for donation, minutes quickly turn into hours before I hear a car pull into the driveway. I expect it to be Morgan but am surprised when I pull back the curtains and see Mom and Cliff walking hand in hand toward the front door looking like a couple of teenagers. A small secret smile graces my face as I wonder how they managed to keep their little love affair a secret from me for so long. I take a deep breath, walk to the front door and open it before Mom has a chance to knock. "Hi, Mom, Cliff. I'm so happy to see you both. What are you doing here?" I ask.

"We thought it was a nice day to get some fresh air and do some visiting. We just left Aunt Sue and thought we'd stop in here and say hello to you."

"Well, great, come on in. I was just going through some old clothes trying to figure out what to keep and what to donate. Can I get you both something to drink?"

"Coffee would be nice," Mom says.

As I pull out three coffee cups from an open box in the kitchen, Cliff walks around the living room and eyes the other packed boxes scattered about the room. "It looks like you're ready to move into your new apartment, Adele."

"Yes," I say as I push the button for the first cup of coffee to brew. "All I need now is to wait until the fifteenth of August for the closing and then move in."

"So you were able to convince the owners of the apartment to let you move in prior to September 1st?" Mom asks.

"Yes, Barbara did," I say. "Apparently they may have to finish painting a few rooms after I move in but that's no big deal. You know I don't mind the smell of paint."

Once all three cups of coffee are finished brewing, I carry them to the kitchen table where I invite Mom and Cliff to join me. We sip our coffee yet no one speaks. I decide it is up to me to break the ice. "So, the man I have been dating, Morgan Spencer, will be here shortly."

Mom sets down her coffee cup. "You've been dating a man by the name of Morgan *Spencer*?"

"Yes, Mom, I have," I say bravely as I take another sip of my coffee.

"For how long?" she asks.

"Since about four weeks ago, a little less than you and Cliff have been dating I guess."

Mom picks up her cup once again and is silenced, momentarily.

"About that," Cliff says. "We never meant to hide our relationship from you, Adele. It's just, well, after Spencer died and Lonnie left we weren't sure how much more you could take. We didn't want to upset you."

I smile over the rim of my coffee cup, "you'd be surprised at how much I can take, Cliff."

"Yes, you've always been very brave," Mom says as she smiles in my direction.

Just then the sound of the doorbell pulls me from my

seat and it is excuse enough for me to stand, leaving the inevitable conversation hanging in the air for a little while longer.

I open the door, expecting to find Morgan but am dumb struck to find Maria instead. Quickly, without thinking, I shut the door and leave her standing alone on the front porch.

Mom and Cliff join my side. "What's going on Adele," Mom asks.

"It's just a woman that I don't want to talk to right now. I just need her to go away."

"Should I speak to her?" Cliff asks.

"No. That's not necessary. Listen, I'm sorry, please just make yourselves comfortable for a few minutes longer while I step outside and talk to her, okay?"

"Are you sure everything is going to be alright?" Mom asks. "Who is she?"

"She's just a woman from the support group at Children's Hospital," I lie. "Don't worry, everything is fine. Seeing her here just startled me at first but I can talk to her now, just give me a few minutes."

"Alright, if you say so," Mom says as she and Cliff walk back into the kitchen while I step out onto the front porch.

I am startled to see how much Maria resembles Morgan. Up close, I see his eyes staring back at me. Same smile, same nose, same chin.

"Maria, this has got to stop!" I snap. "If you don't leave me in peace I will call the police."

"Good," Maria says. "Call the police." Saliva gurgles in her cheeks and she slurs her words, "It's Morgan, Adele. He's not right. He'll hurt you. You need to stay away from him. I'm here to warn you."

"Stop it, Maria!" I say again in a hushed tone. "Your family told me all about you. They said you would try to do this and I won't have it! Just go back to wherever it is you came from and leave me alone."

Moments later Cliff opens the door and asks if everything is okay.

"Yes, Maria is just leaving," I say and Maria begrudgingly stomps off of the porch and jumps back onto her bicycle and rides away.

"What was that all about?" Cliff asks.

"Nothing, really. She's a little sick upstairs," I say as I draw circles in the air around my head.

"Are you sure everything is going to be okay? She looked a little weird."

"She is weird, but harmless," I lie. Cliff and I walk back inside and join Mom at the kitchen table for a game of scrabble.

Soon Morgan arrives and joins us. His dauntless and endearing charm wins Mom and Cliff over immediately as he begins to tell us about his day, less any mention of Cleveland. We spend the next few hours getting to know each other better and set a date for next Saturday night to go out for dinner. Morgan tells us he will take care of making a reservation at his favorite restaurant in the city, Pastabilities, and I forget for a while about Maria.

The light of day has passed when it finally comes time for Mom and Cliff to leave. As we step outside, the once bright sky has been replaced with a thousand blossoming stars that blaze a trail across the night sky. It's an unusually warm night, we notice, as Morgan and I wave good-bye and close the front door. "It's warm enough to sleep outside tonight. Are you game?" Morgan asks.

"Outside? Where?"

"At my place," he says. "I have a tent. We can put it up out back along the lake. And I have some wine and some sleeping bags and some wine...."

"Okay, I get it," I say as I let out a hardy laugh. "It sounds like fun. Most of my stuff is packed anyway, so let's go."

Morgan turns on the radio in the car and we listen as the reporter announces that a previous person of interest in regards to Valerie's disappearance has been ruled out based on lack of evidence. I turn to Morgan and ask, "Are they talking about you?"

"Yes, they are," Morgan says as he makes the turn down the dirt road leading to his cottage.

"Well, you certainly waited a long time to tell me this."

"But you knew I was innocent, right?"

"Of course, but it's nice to know that the police now think so too."

"You're right, I should have told you sooner, when I found out a few days ago. Based on my recent behavior the night you found me in a drunken stupor, we weren't exactly on the best speaking terms on this topic."

"I see your point," I say. "I'm just glad that the police are no longer interested in you."

"Me, too," Morgan says as he pulls into his driveway and we hop out of the car.

"Maria stopped by my house tonight, said she wanted to warn me about you," I say.

"Jesus, Adele, why didn't you tell me this sooner?!"

"I couldn't exactly tell you about it in front of Mom and Cliff. This is the first opportunity I've had," I say, as we walk into the house together.

"So what happened?"

"Nothing, really. After a brief conversation I told her to

go away then Cliff stepped outside and I think he scared her away. She got onto her bike and rode off."

"Goddam her!" Morgan thunders. "When will it ever end?"

"When she is arrested for the murder of Valerie Dunne, I suppose," I say as Morgan goes deaf and dumb. "So what about you?"

Morgan opens the front hall closet and pulls down two sleeping bags and hands them to me.

"What about me?" he asks.

"Did you find Cleveland?"

"Yes."

"And *you* are just telling me about this *now*?"

"I guess we're even," he says but I am not amused. "So, tell me, what did he have to say?"

"He said he doesn't know you or anything about what Carl was doing before his death."

"Great. Do you believe him?"

"I'm afraid so. He seemed like a pretty standup guy, considering his line of work."

"Now what?" I ask.

"I'm not sure, but I'm going to talk to Dixon. I think he knows more than he's letting on."

"Really?"

"Well, I'm not sure but I've got a hunch. It's worth a shot anyway. I'll stay on top of him."

I carry the sleeping bags outside while Morgan starts putting up the poles for the tent. "Morgan, did I ever tell you what Carl said to me about the hit man the first day I met him?"

"No."

"Well, after I asked him if it would be him, he said it wouldn't and that he would never tell me the hit man's name."

"Right, you told me that part."

"Well, for a minute I thought he was going to tell me so I stopped him from saying anymore. I said something like, 'don't tell me his name, I don't want to know."

"I'm listening," Morgan says as he continues to work on the tent.

"Carl asked me why I was so sure it would be a man."

"Interesting," Morgan says as he looks up at me from a knelt position. "But what are you getting to?"

I hand him the sleeping bags and he unrolls them inside of the tent. "Nothing, I was just thinking out loud."

As I climb into the tent, Morgan lights a lantern that flickers in the darkness and casts dance-like shadows across the walls.

"So you think the hit man could be a woman?" Morgan asks.

"Maybe."

"Interesting," he says again as I lay back onto the ground.

"It's quite the coincidence that Maria went to school in Utica, don't you think?"

Morgan gives me a look of concern but quickly changes the subject. "Listen, Adele, you're letting your mind run away from you. It's late and you've had a very trying couple of days. Let's just try not to worry about this anymore tonight, okay?"

"Okay, you're right," I say, knowing full well that sleep will not come easily tonight as I close my eyes and listen to the sounds, imaginary or real, outside of the tent. *Are those footsteps?*

* * *

Five hours later I wake to the smell of bacon frying outside. Everything is fresh and dewy and still expect for the gentle sounds of the waves crashing on the shore of the lake. I peek outside of the tent and find the fire on the gas grill snapping and popping, flinging sparks left and right as Morgan drops four eggs into a cast iron pan. "I figured we could have our breakfast out here too," Morgan says as I join him next to the picnic table. "How did you sleep?" he asks.

"Okay. Would you like me to make some coffee?"

"Already made," he says as he points to the blue and white speckled urn resting on the table. "Would you prefer one lump or two?" he asks, in his best British accent.

"None for me, kind sir," I say. "I'll take my coffee black with no sugar, as usual, please."

"Coming right up," he says as he pulls out two matching blue and white speckled tin cups and pours the piping hot goodness.

"How long have you been up?" I ask.

"For about an hour," he says as he skillfully flips over the eggs in the sizzling pan. He then grabs a pot holder to protect his hand as he lifts a hot lid from another pot revealing four scrumptious-looking buttermilk biscuits.

"This is amazing," I say. "Best sleep over ever!"

"Thank you," Morgan says as he serves me two eggs with a side of bacon and a fresh hot biscuit.

Together, as we eat on Onondaga's northern shore, we watch as sunlight flickers across the lake, twisting and turning the waves which sparkle like a thousand of brilliant white diamonds. "We should do this more often," I say as I finish my biscuit.

"We should," Morgan says as he takes his last bite and

stands to clear the table. I help him carry the dishes inside to be washed just as the rustling wind fills the trees with the whispering scent of the lake.

Once all of the dishes are dropped into the sink, Morgan lifts his guitar from its cradle and begins to play a new song. Something I don't recognize but lovely all the same. "That's beautiful," I say. "What is that?"

"I wrote it for you, Adele," he says.

"Does it have any words?" I ask.

"Almost," he says. "But I'm not quite finished writing them yet."

Once again, he draws me close and I feel the lazy rays of Sunday take over my heart and mind as I melt into his embrace. "I feel like I have known you my entire life, Mr. Spencer."

"Maybe you have," he says. "My mother believes in reincarnation."

"Maybe she's right," I say as he carries me into the bedroom, and we experience another day of uninterrupted love.

32.

An unseasonably cold and wet evening blows in from Canada as we drive into Syracuse for dinner the following Friday night. The temperature has dropped almost twenty degrees since yesterday and it feels like an early fall. Mom, Cliff and I step out of my car and walk under the cover of our umbrellas three short blocks to the restaurant where we are to meet Morgan by 7:00 p.m.

When we arrive, we are seated in a room off to the right. Once an abandoned warehouse, the modern restaurant features exposed brick walls, stainless steel accents, hardwood floors, and retro lighting fixtures. The atmosphere is chic and lighthearted and a live jazz band plays softly in the background. "Do you like jazz, Cliff?" I ask.

"Yes, in fact I do," Cliff says as he pulls out a chair for Mom to sit.

"Then we're both in luck, me too," I say when our waitress arrives at our table. "What would you like to drink, Mom?"

"I'm not sure; maybe a glass of white wine would be nice?"

I turn to the waitress. "What type of Riesling do you carry?"

"We have two, both Finger Lakes wines. One is from Lamoreaux Landing and the other..."

"Stop," I say abruptly. "My mother and I will each have a glass of the Lamoreaux Riesling. Mom, you will love it. Morgan brought a bottle over to the house a few weeks ago and it was spectacular."

"I'll have a light beer, a draft please," Cliff adds.

"What kind?" The waitress asks.

"Surprise me," Cliff says as he smiles and his blue eyes twinkle in the soft light.

After the waitress leaves, I look down at my watch; 7:15. "I'm not sure what's keeping Morgan," I say. "But we can go ahead and order some appetizers if you'd like. I heard their stretch bread is wonderful. They make it fresh here every morning."

"Let's wait a little bit longer, dear," Mom says. "I'm sure he'll be along any minute."

The waitress returns with our drinks as my phone begins to jingle. "That's probably him now," I say as I grab my phone. After I read his text message I power down my phone and look across the table. "He can't make it."

"Has something happened?" Mom gasps.

"No, not really. Apparently he's swamped at work and can't get away. He's still at the shop."

"That's all right, Adele, we'll have a good time without him. Just the three of us," Cliff reassures me as he reaches his hand across the table and rests it on top of mine.

"Right, no worries," Mom says and I agree so we order the house specialty appetizer; stretch bread paired with their famous spicy hot tomato oil for dipping.

"Do you like the wine, Mom?"

"Yes, it's wonderful, great choice," Mom says as she clears her voice and smiles at me. "Now, Adele, tell me, has Morgan ever been married?"

"Jeez, Mom, subtle," I say as I take another sip of my wine, but I really don't mind. Naturally Mom wants to learn more about the man I'm dating. "Yes," I say. "But I'm afraid it's not a very happy story."

"How so?" Mom asks.

"Well, his wife, Gloria, and their young child; a girl by the name of Waverly, were killed in a tragic car accident ten years ago."

"Oh, poor Morgan," Mom says. "He must have been devastated."

"Yes, he was," I say. "But he has learned to move on which has helped me tremendously. He sets a good example."

I think about telling them about the bracelet I made for Waverly but I'm sure it would take too much explanation and quickly abandon the idea. Besides, it is kind of weird and I don't want to portray Morgan in the wrong light.

"So how is your new intern working out?" Mom asks.

"Oh, Ellie? She is wonderful. The second best decision I've made in regards to the boutique; Orlando being the first," I say as I pull off a section of stretch bread and sop up some of the delicious spicy oil. "What I especially like about having Ellie on board is that I don't have all of the responsibility for the jewelry making. It's very nice."

"I'm sure it is," Cliff says. "So are you all set for your closing next week?"

"Yes, can you believe it's almost here? Time flies," I say as I think about Labor Day quickly approaching, too.

"Wait 'til you get to be our age!" Mom says, and we all laugh.

Over dinner; chicken riggies all around, an Upstate specialty, we comment to one another on how Pastabilities has lived up to its reputation; our meal is spectacular, even without Morgan's company.

As we leave the restaurant, we each zip our jackets tightly as we walk back to my car. Mom lives a short ten minute drive from downtown, so I have them delivered home safely in no time.

"Thank you, Adele, for being our chauffer tonight," Cliff jokes as he and Mom get out of the car and say good-night.

"Good night," I say and pull away.

Although I understand that work comes first, I'm secretly a little angry with Morgan for not showing up tonight, so I decide not to drive by his cottage. Maybe it's the wine doing the thinking now, but I decide I'm going to drive out to the Lounge and have a look around. Maybe Morgan is right and Dixon knows more than he's letting on. I can be very persuasive, I remind myself, especially with men, so I decide to give it try.

By the time I reach Utica, its half past ten and the Lounge is packed. Just another Friday night, I suppose, as I cross the street and enter the familiar bar.

As always, the room is deathly dark and the music is terribly loud. Habitually, my skin begins to crawl but luckily, Dixon is behind the bar and he gives me a quick wink, calming my nerves. He then holds up two limes, one in each hand, and asks, "the usual?"

"Yes, how did you know?" I tease.

"That's what they pay me for, beautiful."

When my drink arrives, I ask Dixon if he's heard anything more about Carl and the unfinished business I had with him.

"No," Dixon says, "But Cleveland is sitting in the room out back. You should go talk to him."

"I don't think he knows anything," I say. "Morgan has already spoken to him."

"Oh, really, when?" Dixon asks.

"About a week ago," I say. "Why?"

"Because Cleveland just got in from Buffalo this morning. He's been gone for about two weeks."

"Really," I say. "But that can't be right. I'm sure it was only a week ago that Morgan spoke to him."

"Then they must have met in Buffalo because I'm telling ya, lime juice, Cleveland hasn't been around."

I feel myself about to burst with rage and hurt but I manage to compose myself. There must be some sort of mistake. *Why would Morgan lie to me about speaking to Cleveland?* Christ, my life is at stake! There has to be more to the story. "Can I just go out back and introduce myself?" I ask.

"Sure, but they're playing poker so Cleveland may ask you to wait it out."

"No problem," I say. "I've got all the time in the world for Cleveland."

The back room is thick with nicotine from both cigars and cigarettes and if it wasn't for the liquid courage running through my veins I'm sure I would not be able to walk into such a room all alone. But I must speak to Cleveland, tonight.

As I look around the room, I see three different tables with active poker games and it occurs to me that I don't know what Cleveland looks like. Just then Dixon enters the room from a back door leading from the bar and motions for me to step over to the second table. "Adele, this is Cleveland," Dixon says as he points to a large man sitting at the table in front of him as I let loose a nervous smile.

Cleveland is much younger than I imagined; probably about 38 or 40. He has a shaved head, a thick, black goatee and a very handsome face. He drinks a tomato drink with a stalk of celery and gives me a wink. "Well, hello, Adele. My night is looking up, hey fellas?" he says as the table erupts with laughter and suddenly reeks of male bravado.

I want to shrink into a miniature creature, but I stand tall and ask if he has a few minutes to speak to me. "In private," I add.

"Sure, I wanted out of this stinkin' game anyway," he says as he throws in his hand as the other men moan.

"Nice timing, sweetheart," I hear one of the men yell as more laughter erupts. Cleveland and I leave the room and walk into the main section of the bar. We take a seat in a booth, not far from where I first met Carl and, again, the hairs on the back of my neck stand in full attention. I swirl my drink around with my straw as Cleveland examines his cell phone for a few minutes. Once he sets it down, I feel that it's my turn to speak.

"Cleveland, my name is Adele Hamilton and I wanted to ask you a few questions about Carl Nardone."

"Are you a cop?"

I can't help myself, I giggle. "God, no," I say. "I can't imagine anything worse than being a cop."

"Okay, what do you want to know about Carl? I suppose you know he's dead, right?"

"Yes, I know. That's why I wanted to talk to you. But, before I begin, do you remember talking to man in here about a week ago by the name of Morgan?" I ask.

"No, sure don't," Cleveland says. "I was out of town on business a week ago. Why? Who's Morgan?"

"Never mind, it's not important," I say as I bite my bottom lip and do my best not to scream. "So, as I was saying, I had some interrupted business with Carl and now that he is no longer with us I'm not sure who to turn to."

"What kind of business?" Cleveland asks.

"The worst kind of business," I say.

"Look, lady, I'd like to help you but if you can't be more specific I'm not sure how I can."

He's right, I need to tell him everything. He may be the hit man and as creepy as it is to be sitting down with the man that may be scheduled to kill me soon, I have to take a leap of faith. "Alright, I'll tell you," I say as I finish my drink. "I'm not proud of this, but you have to understand, when I first met with Carl, several weeks ago, I was beyond depressed. I was suicidal."

"You? Doesn't fit," Cleveland says with a shrug of his shoulders.

"That's what Carl said."

"Smart man, go on."

I reach into the bottom of my glass and pull out a chunk of ice and pop it into my mouth. "When I met with Carl, I gave him a large sum of money."

"So the plot thickens," Cleveland says as he pulls out a pack of cigarettes from his shirt pocket. "Do you mind if I smoke?"

"No, go right ahead."

"How much money?" he asks.

"I'm not sure that matters but it was a lot, ten thousand dollars."

"I see," Cleveland says as he blows smoke out of the side of his mouth. "And what did Carl promise you in exchange for this large sum of money?"

"I ordered a hit on myself. I wanted to die, but I was too much of a sissy to kill myself," I say as I lean forward in the booth and rest my elbows on the table and cross my fingers in front of my face.

Cleveland begins to chuckle and I want to slap him. *How can he laugh at a time like this?* "Let me guess," Cleveland says. "You've changed your mind?"

"Yes, can you help me? Is it you? If so, you can keep the money. I don't want it. I just want my life back."

"Lady, I wish I could help you but this is the first I've heard of this," he says, as he takes a chomp of his celery stick."

"Is there anyone else that might know something about it?" I ask.

"Not that I know of," Cleveland says. "Carl made his own arrangements but, hell; you're still here so maybe..."

"No. That's just the thing. I asked that I not be killed until Labor Day weekend; I had some loose ends to tie up first, but now that Labor Day is only three weeks away the clock is ticking."

Cleveland leans back in the booth, scratches his head and looks off to one side as he thinks. "The only thing I know is that Carl had a girlfriend. A weirdo with dark hair. That's all I know."

"What kind of weirdo?" I ask as my pulse quickens.

"Just a weirdo," Cleveland says. "Not much more I can say, that's all I know."

"Does she come in here?"

"She used to, but I haven't seen her around since Carl died."

"Does the name 'Maria' ring a bell?"

Cleveland squints and cracks his knuckles above his head as if he's trying to remember the girl's name. "No, I'm sorry, it doesn't," he says as he stands. "I wish I could help you, Adele, but I don't know her name or anything more."

"Thanks," I say as I stand to leave wondering whether or not I ever want to see Morgan again.

33.

    I rise slowly out of my bed and drag myself into the shower. I have a pounding headache, but I need to go shopping. Tomorrow is Orlando's birthday, and I am planning a small get together for him down at the boutique. Normally, I would throw a party at my house but with everything still in boxes, it makes better sense to go downtown.

    As I stand in the shower and let the hot water beat down on top of my aching head, I once again think about Ellie and how grateful I am to have her working with us. Normally, by this time on a Saturday morning, I would be down at the boutique slouched over my work station trying to come up with the next best thing in jewelry design. Sometimes I wonder if I've placed too much stress on the young girl but she really seems to enjoy the free reign I've allowed her and it shows. Her jewelry is selling rapidly and we are making a lot of money.

    After I am toweled off, I reach into a large box and I fish around until I find a pair of faded old jeans and a light blue tunic and get dressed. I pull my hair back with a rubber band and throw on an Alfred U baseball cap which allows my pony tail to flow freely through the opening in the back. After I spray on a little light perfume and apply some lip gloss, I turn off the lights, leave my bedroom and enter the kitchen.

    I didn't give Mom an exact time for me to pick her up so I figure I can have a slice of toast with some peanut butter before I leave. As I fumble through the boxes in the kitchen, looking for the toaster, my phone rings to the tune of *Into the Mystic* and I let it go to message. I haven't decided yet what I'm going to say to Morgan the next time I speak to him. I can't imagine why he would lie to me about meeting Cleveland, and I'm not sure I can ever forgive him. This is my life we are talking about here. *What was he thinking?*

After my toast pops up, I grab the peanut butter and slather a healthy amount over my slice of bread and take a bite. I love peanut butter. It comforts me. A pile of mail is stacked on the end of the counter so I begin going through it as my phone rings. Again, I ignore it (Morgan) and push the button for my coffee. While I wait, I look around the kitchen for my travel mug. I can't wait to get settled into my new apartment. Living out of these boxes is beginning to drive me crazy. After several more frustrating minutes of searching, I finally find the mug and transfer the hot coffee into it. Finished with my toast, I get ready to head out to Mom's when I remember my shopping list in the bedroom.

As I walk into the bedroom and reach for the list, I notice the bedroom window is open and the curtain is blowing outward. The screen is also missing.

Someone has been here!

I run to the window and stick my head outside and look around. I see no one but I close the window and lock it, then check to make sure that the other two windows are locked. They are. I begin to shiver and sit down on the bed while my heart seems to pound outside of my chest. I look around the room. Nothing looks out of place or out of the ordinary until I notice a small box on the chair next to the window. I grab it and open it up when an overwhelming stench seeps into the room, choking me, and I am certain I am going to be sick. The smell is like nothing I've ever smelled before. Like something dead. I hold my breath and pick up what's wrapped tightly inside and toss the box. I find layer after layer of tissue paper wrapped in more layers of tape. I think I'm never going to find anything but I continue to rip it open. When I finally get to the center I begin to tremble. Covered in slime and caked with blood are the remains of Wellington's two gouged out eyeballs.

I drop the package and begin to scream louder than I have ever screamed in my life and then throw up all over myself. Still trembling, I try to run from the room, but my steps are unsteady and I stumble about until I finally reach the kitchen where I find my phone. I select Morgan's name from my many contacts and pray he picks up.

"Adele, I'm so glad..."

"Morgan!" I scream. "Maria...has been...here...you need to come...Wellington's eyes..."

"Lock all the windows and doors. I'll be right there," he says as I throw the phone across the room. I drop to the floor where I curl up into a fetal position. As if it will make it all better, and help erase the stench still emanating from the bedroom.

I wait what seems to be an eternity until I hear Morgan's car finally pull up out front. I manage to lift myself off of the kitchen floor and stagger to the front window where I look outside to be certain it is him. When I open the door I'm still covered in my own vomit. Morgan steps inside and tells me to wait by the front door while he searches the house; baseball bat in hand.

After Morgan is certain no one is left inside and the house is secure, I strip off my clothing and step into the shower and lather feverishly from head to toe. I stand under the scalding water to rinse away the fear for what must be a good fifteen or twenty minutes. I try to erase the images burned into my mind of Wellington's eyes and the smell on my entire body until my flesh is raw and bright red. After several more futile minutes of scrubbing, Morgan taps gently on the bathroom door and asks if I'm alright.

"I'll be right out," I say, even though I never want to get out of this shower again. But once I do, I wrap a towel around myself and walk into the living room where Morgan is standing near the window.

"I cleaned everything up, sprayed some Lysol around and opened the windows in your room again," Morgan says as he finally takes me into his arms. "We need to let the place air out."

"She's sick!" I say. "Who does something like that?"

"I don't know but she won't come back here once she sees my car."

"This can't go on. We need to do something!"

"I know," Morgan says. "I'm going to talk to my parents, today. I think it's time we think about going to the police."

"Good!" I say. "Because if you don't, I will!"

Morgan releases me. "Adele, please don't do anything before I have a chance to talk to them. Promise me."

"I can't stay here another night," I say. "Can I stay with you?"

"Yes, of course," he says.

"I also don't think I can go back into that bedroom. Do you think you can find me something else to wear?"

"Like what?"

"Anything, a pair of jeans and a top. I don't care but I need to get dressed and call my mother. I was supposed to pick her up so we could go shopping together for Orlando. Tomorrow...his birthday...I'm...supposed to be..." I can't even get the words out before I begin to sob uncontrollably.

"Adele, do you have anything in the house to calm your nerves?"

"Yes, some Valium. It's in my makeup case on the nightstand. Could you get it for me?"

Morgan leaves me and walks back into the bedroom. A few minutes later he returns with a dark blue pair of jeans a red top and the bottle of Valium. I get dressed in the living room while Morgan gets me a bottle of water from the refrigerator. "Thanks, Morgan," I say as I swallow two pills and drink the entire bottle of water.

"Do you think you can go shopping?"

"No, not after this kicks in, I'll be out for a couple of hours."

"Well, you need to call your mother before you do so she doesn't worry."

"What should I tell her?" I ask.

"Tell her you think you've come down with something and will have to go shopping later after you rest. Do you think you can do that, Adele?"

"Yes," I say. "After I get some sleep I should be okay, but, please, will you stay with me?"

"Yes. After you fall asleep I'll call the folks and discuss with them what needs to be done."

"Thank you, Morgan."

"You're welcome," he says as he helps me to the sofa and covers me with a light blanket. After I've reassured my mother everything is fine, I fall to sleep almost immediately, resorting to my old coping mechanism – thinking about Spencer until the magic of him enters my dreams.

34.

The next morning I wake in the warmth of Morgan's bed. The air is cool from the breeze blowing off the lake and I think about rolling over and going back to sleep, but I wrap my bathrobe tightly around my body and step outside onto the back deck.

Orlando's party is taking place later today, and Mom and Ellie have assured me that they have taken care of all the remaining details. The forty miniature cupcakes have been delivered by the baker, the champagne and orange juice are chilling in the refrigerator at the boutique, Wegmans will be delivering a veggie, shrimp and sandwich platter soon, and the gifts are all in place. I feel terrible about having to lie to Mom and Ellie about being ill yesterday – when I wasn't – but if I were to tell Mom what's happening with Maria she would probably have another stroke. Also, I never told her, or anyone, about how I found Wellington lying dead in the garage with his eyes gouged out. Everyone just assumed he died of old age, and I let them.

Morgan steps out onto the deck and hands me a cup of hot coffee.

"Thank you," I say. "Have you been up long?"

"About three hours," he says as he takes a seat next to me. "Is everything set for the party?"

"Yes, thanks to Mom and Ellie." I take a sip of my coffee. "Did you talk to your parents yesterday about Maria?"

"Not exactly."

"What does that mean?"

"I called Dad, but he and Mother drove up to New

Hampshire for the weekend so he wanted me to wait until they return on Monday."

"And what am I supposed to do in the meantime, hope that she doesn't kill me?"

"She won't kill you, Adele. You'll be with me until we get this whole thing sorted out."

I look out onto the lake and decide to wait until later tonight, after the party, to discuss Cleveland. I'm simply not in the mood. I'm emotionally exhausted and a bit too angry with him still to have a good conversation right now. It will have to wait.

* * *

Later, after I am dressed for the party in a short black and blue paisley print dress, black tights and boots, I find Morgan in the bedroom fumbling through a few folders in his file cabinet. I look down at my watch; 3:45 p.m. "Are you ready?" I ask. "We need to be at the boutique by four."

"Yes, I'm ready," he says as he closes the cabinet and turns around. He holds his hands out to his side and spins around for my inspection. Dressed in a pair of light gray linen trousers, a crisp white cotton shirt and a pair of faded brown loafers he looks to be about twenty-five years old.

"Beautiful," I say with a smile.

"Then let's go," Morgan says as he locks the door behind us, and we walk to his car.

When we arrive downtown, Mom, Ellie, Aunt Sue and Cliff are waiting for us and they have taken the liberty of hanging some "Happy 40th Birthday" signs strategically throughout the square leading to the boutique. "Was this your idea, Ellie?"

"Yes, do you think Orlando will be okay with it?"

"Of course he will. You know how much he loves being the center of attention. It's perfect!"

"Thank you," Ellie says, and I give her a hug. "How are you feeling today?"

"Much better, thanks to you and Mom. I'm not sure what I would have done without your help. I never could have pulled this off the way I was feeling yesterday," I say as I look back at Morgan.

"What time will Orlando and his partner be here?" Cliff asks.

"We expect them at five so we have plenty of time to wrap his presents and have a few drinks before they arrive," I say.

Sure enough, a few minutes after five, Orlando and his partner, Mitchell, show up and we all fuss over Orlando while he opens his presents and tries not to cry. The last gift he opens is from me and it's the blank onyx ring that Ellie made with the lions carved onto the shoulders, perfect for Orlando, the Leo. "Thank you, Deli. You knew I wanted this ring! And look," he says as he places it on his right ring finger. "It fits me perfectly!"

"You're welcome, Orlando," I say as I laugh and give him a loving embrace. "I love you, partner."

"I love you, too, Deli girl. Thank you for everything, the ring, the party, the signs..."

"You need to thank Ellie for the signs, they were her doing."

"I knew I liked you, too, Ellie," Orlando says and Ellie smiles and nods her head.

As the party is winding down, Cliff pulls me into the work room. "May I speak with you for a minute, Adele?"

"Yes, of course, Cliff. What is it?"

"Well, this may not be the right time to bring it up but

with all this love and goodwill flowing I figured I'd say something to you now." Cliff seems unlike himself, he fidgets and rubs his hands together and it unnerves me.

"Is something wrong?" I ask.

"No, quite the contrary," he says. "Everything is wonderful and with your permission I'd like to ask your mother to marry me."

I let out a sound something like a cackle as I grab him around the shoulders and hug him tightly. "Oh, Cliff! That's fantastic news! Of course! When will you pop the question?"

"Well, I'm thinking about doing it right now. Would that be okay with you?"

"Oh my, yes! But wait, let me get my phone. I have to get a picture of Mom's reaction!"

After I have my phone in hand, Cliff and I walk back out into the showroom and I find my mother looking as lovely as a brand new kitten. Tears are already beginning to form in the corner of my eyes but I hold back, not wanting to spoil the surprise.

Cliff picks up his glass of champagne and taps a fork to its side, quieting the room. He then bends down on one knee in front of where Mom sits, and I know I'm going to cry when Cliff begins to speak. "All love that has not friendship for its base is like a mansion built upon the sand. Ella Wilcox said that and I couldn't agree more. Sarah, we have been friends for many, many years."

"Yes," Mom says as I snap a shot of Cliff kneeling in front of her.

Cliff continues, "And I love you. If you feel the same, could you, would you, my love, consider being my wife? If so, my arms will be your shelter; my heart will be your home."

Aunt Sue, Ellie and Orlando pull out their cell phones, too, tears running down their cheeks, and begin snapping pictures of the lovely couple. I can't remember when a night has ever been so complete.

"I already said 'yes', you idiot," Mom says as she throws her arms around Cliff and we all begin to cry, less one, Morgan.

35.

For the first time since I've known Morgan, I cannot find the words to express how I feel. On one hand, I want to ask him about Cleveland and why he lied to me, but on the other hand, I don't. I want to go on believing that he is flawless but it has become perfectly clear that he is not.

As he drives, I hang my head out the window and let the cool breeze blow across my face as the city, a carnival of lights, slowly fades away. The night air takes me to a state of Nirvana as I close my eyes and try to make it all go away. I'm exhausted worrying about the hit man, Maria and now Morgan's enormous lie. I want to forget my troubles for a little while longer so I allow myself to float on an imaginary cloud and let the wind swallow me up.

Soon the car stops, and the ugly silence between us lingers as we walk single file up the cobblestone path. A hoot owl laments in the night sky. It sounds like broken wind chimes through the frosty air when Morgan turns around and says, "It's getting cold."

I nod, enter the cottage behind him and drop my bag on the floor. "Morgan, I need to talk to you..."

Morgan holds his finger to his lips and makes a hushing sound. "Do you hear that," he whispers.

"What?"

My eyes grow wider as Morgan grabs a butcher knife off of the kitchen table and motions for me to stand still.

"What is it?" I whisper.

"I don't know. Be quiet."

Morgan walks into the bedroom, leaving me alone in the living room where my toes curl into balls as I strain my neck to listen. "Morgan?" I whisper, when I hear the flip of a switch and light suddenly floods the room.

"Gotcha!" Morgan yells as an animal screams in pain and a scuffle ensues. Seconds later he emerges triumphant carrying what appears to be a dead raccoon in his bare hands.

"You killed it?" I ask as blood drips from its carcass, a deep wound to its neck.

"Yes, of course I killed it."

"You probably shouldn't be handling it with you bare hands."

"Could you just get me a trash bag?"

I turn on the light in the kitchen and search for the trash bags. I find one under the sink. "Here," I say as I hold it out at arm's length and turn my face from the bloody scene.

"Jesus, Adele, hold it open!"

Startled, I do as he says and spread it open. He deposits the thirty pound creature into the bag, and it drops to the floor with a thump. I release my hold and run into the bathroom, locking the door behind me. My hands are shaking and I feel raw, numb. I sit down on the side of the tub and breathe in and out, in and out, and then reach for my makeup bag. As I search for the bottle of Valium my fingers find the edges of an envelope instead. I pull it out and see my name written across the top. Agitated, I tear it open.

> *Adele*
> *You need to get out of this house! My brother is a very dangerous man. I know he's told you I'm crazy, but he wants you to believe this so that you don't trust me. Please, I'm begging you, don't trust him! Get out of the house. I'll be waiting.*
> *Maria*
> *P.S. Check the file cabinet.*

I rip the note into a dozen tiny pieces and flush it down

the toilet as I hear Morgan at the bathroom door. I can feel my pulse quicken and my vision blur. *I'll be waiting? Can she really be that sick?*

"Adele, I'm going to go bury this vermin out back but I'll be back," he says and I can't help thinking it sounds more like a threat than a promise as a sibilant sound escapes my lips.

"Okay."

After a few minutes longer, I hear nothing but silence on the other side of the door so I walk into the living room and take a look around. Much to my relief, Morgan and the bag holding the dead raccoon are gone.

The file cabinet?

I walk into the bedroom and try to pull open a drawer but it is locked so I rummage through his desk looking for a key. I find golf balls, paper clips, a stapler, dry cleaning receipts and postage stamps but no key. *Where would he hide a key?*

I walk into the closet and search the upper shelves. Nothing. I try the top drawer of the side table next to the bed, still no luck. *Think!*

And then it dawns on me; the key to the file cabinet must be on the same ring as his house and car keys. *It's hidden in plain sight!* I run into the living room and grab his key chain off of the hutch; car key, house key, but none other.

How long has he been outside? I peek out the window into the back yard. He's shoveling dirt back into a pit. *I need to hurry!* Then I remember, earlier, when he was getting dressed for the party he was rummaging through his file cabinet just before he turned around for my inspection. The key must be near the cabinet. It has to be, so I go back into the bedroom and run my hand along the back of it but find nothing. I look around the floor; still nothing. *Where can it be?* It's got to be on him, in his pants pocket. It's the only reasonable explanation left.

Just then the back door opens, and Morgan is once again inside of the house.

I turn off the light and jump under the covers with my clothes still on and pretend to be asleep when he walks into the bedroom and starts getting undressed. I pray that he leaves the room and he does. He goes into the bathroom and shuts the door. I hear the shower turn on a few seconds later so I know he'll be in there for at least five or ten minutes, maybe more. I jump up, fumble in the dark for his pants and check both pockets. Finally, I find the key. I then kick off my boots and pull my dress up over my head and jump back into bed. The key I've hidden inside one of my boots until later, when he is asleep. When he returns I lie as still as possible. He sees what looks like me sleeping and leaves the bedroom and turns on the TV in the living room.

I wait at least fifteen minutes to be sure he isn't coming back to bed before I slide out from under the covers and dig the key out of my boot. I tiptoe to the bedroom door and peek into the living room. He's lounging in his recliner watching one of his favorite TV cop shows, but it looks like he may fall asleep any minute. Patiently, I wait. Twenty minutes later I hear him snoring so I make my way to the file cabinet.

There is a dim light shining through the sliding glass door which leads to the back porch. It's not very bright but it's enough.

My hands are shaking as I insert the key into the lock. I turn it to the right and the tiny lock snaps open with a *pop!* Nervously, I look over my left shoulder again and listen. He is still sleeping.

There are four drawers, but I open the second, the same one he was in earlier. Inside I find files with people's names written neatly across the top in Morgan's tidy hand writing. I open the first file, Appleton, and find a picture of a motorcycle tank and some receipts for paint and lacquer; a customer of *CarFIX*, no doubt. The next few files are the same, all auto body repair customers. *Maria is crazy.*

Still, I continue to read. After Appleton there are more folders filed alphabetically; Baker, Brady, Dunne, Edison, Grager…

Dunne?

I look over my shoulder again. The TV is still on, and I can clearly hear the sound of him snoring. I flip back to the Dunne folder, open it up and strain my eyes to read. Inside I find naked pictures of Valerie. In one of the pictures, she is tied down to the bed, in this room. I gasp. *Was this a sex act or was she being held captive?* I run my fingers along the Polaroid and trace the outline of her body until I come to her wrist. I see what looks like the dragonfly bracelet, but I can't be sure because it is way too dark. My entire body trembles as my ears begin to ring.

I tiptoe back to the bedroom door and peer out into the living room once more. He is definitely still sleeping. I return to the cabinet.

Carefully, I refile the Dunne folder and read through the next few names when my heart skips a beat. Hamilton. Involuntarily, my teeth begin to chatter. *Breathe. It must be a different Hamilton, it can't be me!* Slowly, I open the folder and an envelope drops out, hitting my toes like a brick. Bending slightly, I see the ladybug doodle flutter in time with my trembling skin, and my worst fears come true. The money, my money, is still stuffed inside. I find my home and work addresses, my photograph. A deep chill runs down my spine, but I have no more time to react as I hear the TV being turned off in the other room.

In one fluid motion, I tuck the folder back into the cabinet and jump into bed as the sound of Morgan's footsteps approach the bedroom door. The key I clutch inside my closed fist. Morgan enters the room, and I can sense him standing over me. "Are you sleeping?" he whispers.

I remain perfectly still.

He turns to walk around to his side of the bed. With his back turned, I open my eyes, briefly, and discover that the file drawer I opened is slightly ajar, the dim light from the back porch shining on it. My heart pounds wildly and my brow perspires.

Don't see it! Don't see it! If he sees it, I'm dead.

He stops, abruptly, and slowly turns toward the sliding glass door, toward the cabinet. As if on a movie screen, in slow motion, he extends his long arm and gently closes the file cabinet drawer. Click! *It's over!* I jump from the bed and start running for the front door, but he overpowers me and spins me around like a top. "Why are you doing this, Morgan?!" I cry. "Please, let me go! You can keep the money! I won't tell anyone, please, just let me go!"

He drags me towards the cabinet. "You think you're so smart, huh Adele? Sneaking around! You stupid little bitch! We had a good thing here!" He puts me in a choke hold, opens the top drawer of the cabinet with his free hand, and fishes around inside. I dig the key into his arm.

He merely laughs as I scream.

A garrote now dangles in his left hand. "Too bad you had to go get all suspicious, Adele; you really have a nice ass. I enjoyed fucking you!" I sink my teeth into his forearm but he barely reacts. "I was even thinking about keeping you around, for a little while longer, at least until winter set in." He pushes me tight up against the file cabinet, his body blocking mine as the garrote brushes my cheek. I kick, I scream and I try to fight him, but he is just too strong. "I must admit, I had a lot of fun with you. Did you like the eyeballs?"

It is all over when I feel the garrote tighten around my neck and I can no longer speak. The pressure increases, and I feel my eyes beginning to roll into the back of my head. I am seconds from unconsciousness, from death, when a volcanic eruption suddenly explodes in my ears and the unimaginable happens: Morgan releases his grip, slumps forward and crashes to the floor. I can barely comprehend what is happening, but I manage to unfurl the garrote and gasp for air. I stumble, then turn to face the sliding glass door. Tears cloud my eyes, but I can clearly see her, standing tall, the light from the back porch shining on her horrified face. She remains frozen in her stance; legs shoulder width apart, a smoking 9mm in her outstretched arms.

I approach her, cautiously, and release the gun from her trembling hands. "You saved my life, Maria."

"I told you not to trust him..."

She slumps to the floor.

"You were right, all along. Thank you."

She nods her head, buries her face into her hands and begins to weep over her brother's dead body while I call the police.

EPILOGUE

Three months later

Thanksgiving is celebrated in my new apartment with the people I love: Mom, Cliff, Aunt Sue, Orlando, Mitchell, Ellie, and my guest of honor, Maria.

I stand and raise my glass high into the air. "This is a day of intense thanks and praise." Everyone smiles. "May we hold tightly to the ones we love, and keep those that are no longer with us forever in our hearts."

We clink our glasses together and sit down to enjoy our enormous feast. We eat, we drink and we laugh into the wee hours of the night until the time comes for everyone to return to their homes.

After the last guest has left, I turn on some music and take a seat on the floor in front of the fireplace with my new kitten, Charlie. The song *1,2,3,4 (I Love You)* comes on and I close my eyes to think about how much Spencer loved this song. I smile and rejoice in his memory, as my hands find their way down the curve of my growing belly. This child will be nothing like his psychopathic father; not with the love I intend to shower over him.

Warm and cozy by the fire, I think about the old blues player in Geneva, happily strumming his Dobro without a single soul around, and I remember what I learned. Sometimes, it's just about the joy that one person can experience, all alone. For me, that really is enough, and I am happy.

THE END

Made in the USA
Middletown, DE
26 March 2016